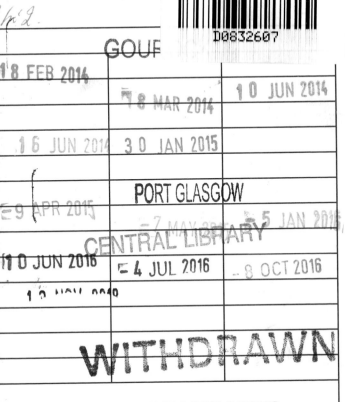

Too angry to stop and clear her vision, she would have walked straight into a wall if someone hadn't reached out and grabbed her by her upper arms.

With a soft gasp Aspen looked up, about to thank whoever had saved her. But the words never came and her quick smile froze on her face as she found herself staring into the hard eyes of a man she had thought she would never see in the flesh again.

The air between them split apart and reformed, vibrating with emotion, as Cruz Rodriguez stared down at her with such cold detachment she nearly shivered.

Eight years dissolved into dust. Guilt, shame, and a host of other emotions all sparked for dominance inside her.

'I...' Aspen blinked, her mind scrambling for poise...words...*something*.

'Hello, Aspen. Nice to see you again.'

From as far back as she can remember **Michelle Conder** dreamed of being a writer. She penned the first chapter of a romance novel just out of high school, but it took much study, many (varied) jobs, one ultra-understanding husband and three very patient children before she finally sat down to turn that dream into a reality.

Michelle lives in Australia, and when she isn't busy plotting loves to read, ride horses, travel and practise yoga.

Recent titles by the same author:

DUTY AT WHAT COST?
LIVING THE CHARADE
HIS LAST CHANCE AT REDEMPTION
GIRL BEHIND THE SCANDALOUS REPUTATION

**Did you know these are also available as eBooks?
Visit www.millsandboon.co.uk**

THE MOST EXPENSIVE LIE OF ALL

BY
MICHELLE CONDER

Published in Great Britain 2014
by Mills & Boon, an imprint of Harlequin (UK) Limited,
Eton House, 18-24 Paradise Road, Richmond, Surrey, TW9 1SR

© 2014 Michelle Conder

ISBN: 978 0 263 24149 5

Printed and bound in Great Britain
by CPI Antony Rowe, Chippenham, Wiltshire

THE MOST
EXPENSIVE LIE
OF ALL

This book is dedicated to Amber and Corin for opening up the world of polo for me and doing it with such warmth and generosity. You guys are great.

To a formidable squash champ, Juan Marcos, who promptly responded to my queries about his game.

And also to my lifelong friend Pam Austin, who wrote down every memory she ever had of her visits to Mexico—which could have been a novel in itself.

Thank you!

CHAPTER ONE

'Eight-three. My serve.'

Cruz Rodriguez Sanchez, self-made billionaire and one of the most formidable sportsmen ever to grace the polo field, let his squash racquet drop to his side and stared at his opponent incredulously. 'Rubbish! That was a let. And it's eight-three *my* way.'

'No way, *compadre*! That was my point.'

Cruz eyeballed his brother as Ricardo prepared to serve. They might only be playing a friendly game of squash but 'friendly' was a relative term between competing brothers. 'Cheats always get their just desserts, you know,' Cruz drawled, moving to the opposite square.

Ricardo grinned. 'You can't win every time, *mi amigo*.'

Maybe not, Cruz thought, but he couldn't remember the last time he'd lost. Oh, yeah, actually he could—because his lawyer was in the process of righting that particular wrong while he blew off steam with his brother at their regular catch-up session.

Feeling pumped, he correctly anticipated Ricardo's attempted 'kill shot' and slashed back a return that his brother had no chance of reaching. Not that he didn't try. His running shoes squeaked across the resin-coated floor as he lunged for the ball and missed.

'*Chingada madre!*'

'Now, now,' Cruz mocked. 'That would be nine-three. My serve.'

'That's just showing off,' Ricardo grumbled, picking himself up and swiping at the sweat on his brow with his sweatband.

Cruz shook his head. 'You know what they say? If you can't stand the heat…'

'Too much talking, *la figura*.'

'Good to see you know your place.' He flashed his brother a lazy smile as he prepared to serve. '*El pequeño*.'

Ricardo rolled his eyes, flipped him the bird and bunkered down, determination etched all over his face. But Cruz was in his zone, and when Ricardo flicked his wrist and sent the ball barrelling on a collision course with Cruz's right cheekbone he adjusted his body with graceful agility and sent the ball ricocheting around the court.

Not bothering to pick himself up off the floor this time, Ricardo lay there, mentally tracking the trajectory of the ball, and shook his head. 'That's just unfair. Squash isn't even your game.'

'True.'

Polo had been his game. Years ago.

Wiping sweat from his face, Cruz reached into his gym bag and tossed his brother a bottle of water. Ricardo sat on his haunches and guzzled it.

'You know I let you win these little contests between us because you're unbearable to be around when you lose,' he advised.

Cruz grinned down at him. He couldn't dispute him. It was a celebrated fact that professional sportsmen were very poor losers, and while he hadn't played professional polo for eight years he'd never lost his competitive edge.

On top of that he was in an exceptionally good mood, which made beating him almost impossible. Remembering the reason for that, he pulled his cell phone from his kitbag to see if the text he was waiting for had come through, frowning slightly when he saw it hadn't.

'Why are you checking that thing so much?' Ricardo queried. 'Don't tell me some *chica* is finally playing hard to get?'

'You wish,' Cruz murmured. 'But, no, it's just a business deal.'

'Ah, don't sweat it. One day you'll meet the *chica* of your dreams.'

Cruz threw him a banal look. 'Unlike you, I'm not looking for the woman of my dreams.'

'Then you'll probably meet her first,' Ricardo lamented.

Cruz laughed. 'Don't hold your breath,' he replied. 'You might meet an early grave.' He tossed the ball in the air and sent it spinning around the court, his concentration a little spoiled by Ricardo's untimely premonition.

Because there *was* a woman. A woman who had been occupying his thoughts just a little too often lately. A woman he hadn't seen for a long time and hoped to keep it that way. Of course he knew why she was jumping into his head at the most inopportune times of late, but after eight years of systematically forcing her out of it that didn't make it any more tolerable.

Not that he allowed himself to get bent out of shape about it. He'd learned early on that the things you were most attached to had the power to cause you the most pain, and since then he'd lived his life very much like a high-rolling gambler—easy come, easy go.

Nothing stuck to him and he stuck to nothing in return—which had, much to everyone's surprise, made him a phenomenally wealthy man.

An 'uneducated maverick', they'd called him. One who had swapped the polo field for the boardroom and invested in deals and stock market bonds more learned businessmen had shied away from. But then Cruz had been trading in the tumultuous early days of the global financial crisis and he'd already lost the one thing he had cared about the most. Defying expectations and market trends seemed inconsequential after that.

What had really fascinated him in the early days was how people had been so ready to write him off because of his Latino blood and his lack of a formal education. What they hadn't realised was that the game of polo had perfectly set him up to achieve in the business world. Killer instincts combined with a tireless work ethic and the ability to think on his feet were all attributes to make you succeed in polo and in business, and Cruz had them in spades. What he didn't have right now—what he *wanted*—was a text from his lawyer advising him that he was the proud owner of one of East Hampton's most prestigious horse studs: Ocean Haven Farm.

Resisting another urge to check his phone, he prowled around the squash court, using the bottom of his sweat-soaked T-shirt to swipe at the perspiration dripping down his face.

'Nice abs,' a feline voice quipped appreciatively through the glass window overlooking the court.

Ah, there she was now.

Lauren Burnside, one of the Boston lawyers he sometimes used for deals he didn't want made public knowledge before the fact, her hip cocked, her expression a smooth combination of professional savvy and sexual knowhow.

'I always thought you were packing a punch beneath all those business suits, Señor Rodriguez. Now I know you are.'

'Lauren.' Cruz let his T-shirt drop and waited for her hot eyes to trail back up to his. She was curvy, elegant and sophisticated, and he had nearly slept with her about a year ago but had baulked at the last minute. He still couldn't figure out why. 'Long way to come to make a house call, counsellor. A text would have sufficed.'

'Not quite. We have a hitch.' She smiled nonchalantly. 'And since I was in California, just a hop, skip and a jump away from Acapulco, I thought I'd deliver the news *mano-a-mano.*' She smiled. 'So to speak.'

Cruz scowled, for once completely unmoved by the flick of her tongue across her glossy mouth.

He knew women found him attractive. He was tall, fit, with straight teeth and nose, a full head of black hair, and he was moneyed-up and uninterested in love. It appeared to be the perfect combination. '*Untameable,*' as one date had purred. He'd smiled, told her he planned to stay that way and she'd come on even stronger. Women, in his experience, were rarely satisfied and usually out for what they could get. If they had money they wanted love. If they had love they wanted money. If they had twenty pairs of shoes they wanted twenty-one. It was tedious in the extreme.

So he ignored his lawyer's honey trap and kept his mind sharp. 'That's not what I want to hear on a deal that was meant to be completed two hours ago, Ms Burnside.' He kept his voice carefully blank, even though his heart rate had sped up faster than during the whole squash game.

'Let me come down.'

For all the provocation behind those words Cruz could tell she had picked up his *not interested* vibe and was smart enough to let it drop.

'She your latest?'

'No.'

Cruz's curt response raised his brother's eyebrows.

'She wants to be.'

Cruz folded his arms as Lauren pushed open the clear door and stepped onto the court, her power suit doing little to disguise the killer body beneath. She inhaled deeply, the smell of male sweat clearly pleasing to her senses.

'You boys have been playing hard,' she murmured provocatively, looking at them from beneath dark lashes.

Okay, so maybe she wasn't that smart. 'What's the hitch?' Cruz prompted.

She raised a well-tended brow at his curtness. 'You don't want to go somewhere more private?'

'This is Ricardo, my brother, and vice-president of Rodriguez Polo Club. I repeat: what's the hitch?'

Lauren's forehead remained wrinkle-free in the face of his growing agitation and he didn't know if that was due to nerves of steel or Botox. Maybe both.

'The hitch,' she said calmly, 'is the granddaughter. Aspen Carmichael.'

Cruz felt his shoulders bunch at the unexpectedness of hearing the name of the female he was doing his best to forget. The last time he'd laid eyes on her she'd been seventeen, dressed in nothing but a nightie and putting on an act worthy of Marilyn Monroe.

The little scheme she and her preppy fiancé had concocted had done Cruz out of a fortune in money and, more importantly, lost him the respect of his family and peers.

Aspen Carmichael had bested him once before and he'd walked away. He'd be damned if he walked away again.

'How?'

'She wants to keep Ocean Haven for herself and her uncle has magnanimously agreed to sell it to her at a reduced cost. The information has only just come to light, but apparently if she can raise the money in the next five days the property is hers.'

Cruz stilled. 'How much of a reduced cost?'

When Lauren named a figure half that which he had offered he cursed loudly. 'Joe Carmichael is not the sharpest tool in the shed, but why the hell would he do that?'

'Family, darling.' Lauren shrugged. 'Don't you know that blood is thicker than water?'

Yes, he did, but what he also knew was that everyone was ultimately out for themselves and if you let your guard down you'd be left with nothing more than egg on your face.

He ran a hand through his damp hair and sweat drops sprayed around his head.

Lauren jumped back as if he'd nearly drenched her designer suit in sulphuric acid and threw an embarrassed glance towards Ricardo, who was busy surveying her charms.

Cruz snapped his attention away from both of them and concentrated on the blank wall covered in streaks of rubber from years of use.

Eight years ago Ocean Haven had been his home. For eleven years he had lived above the main stable and worked diligently with the horses—first as a groom, then as head trainer and finally as manager and captain of Charles Carmichael's star polo team. He'd been lifted from poverty and obscurity in a two-dog town because of his horsemanship by the wealthy American who had spotted him on the *hacienda* where Cruz had been working at the time.

Cruz gritted his teeth.

He'd been thirteen and trying to keep his family from going under after the sudden and pointless death of his father.

Charles Carmichael, he'd later learned, had ambitious plans to one day build a polo 'dream team' to rival all others, and he'd seen in Cruz his future protégé. His mother had seen in him an unmanageable boy she could use to keep the rest of his siblings together. She'd said sending him off with the American would be the best for him. What she'd meant was that it would be the best for all of them, because Old Man Carmichael was paying her a small fortune to take him. Cruz had known it at the time—and hated it—but because he'd loved his family more than anything he'd acquiesced.

And, hell, in the end his mother had been right. By the age of seventeen Cruz had become the youngest player ever to achieve a ten handicap—the highest ranking any player could achieve and one that only a handful ever did. By the age of twenty he'd been touted as possibly the best polo player who had ever lived.

By twenty-three the dream was over and he'd become the joke of the very society who had kissed his backside more times than he cared to remember.

All thanks to the devious Aspen Carmichael. The devious and extraordinarily beautiful Aspen Carmichael. And what shocked Cruz the most was that he hadn't expected it of her. She'd blindsided him and that had made him feel even more foolish.

She had come to Ocean Haven as a lonely, sweet-natured ten-year-old who had just lost her mother in a horrible accident some had whispered was suicide. He'd hardly seen her during those years. His summers had been spent playing polo in England and she had attended some posh boarding school the rest of the year. To him she'd always been a gawky kid with wild blonde hair that looked as if it could use a good pair of scissors. Then one year he'd injured his shoulder and had to spend the summer—her summer break—at Ocean Haven, and *bam!* She had been about sixteen and she had turned into an absolute stunner.

All the boys had noticed and wanted her attention.

So had Cruz, but he hadn't done anything about it. Okay, maybe he'd thought about it a number of times, especially when she had thrown him those hot little glances from beneath those long eyelashes when she assumed he wasn't looking, and, okay, possibly he could remember one or two dreams that she had starred in, but he never would have touched her if she hadn't come on to him first. She'd been too young, too beautiful, too *pure*.

He found himself running his tongue along the edge of

his mouth and the taste of her exploded inside his head. She sure as hell hadn't been pure *that* night.

Gritting his teeth, he shoved her out of his mind. Memory could be as fickle as a woman's nature and his aviator glasses were definitely not rose coloured where she was concerned.

'You okay, *hermano*?'

Cruz swung around and stared at Ricardo without really seeing him. He liked to think he was a fair man who played by the rules. A forgive-and-forget kind of man. He'd stayed away from Ocean Haven and anything related to it after Charles Carmichael had given him the boot. Now his property had come up for sale and objectively speaking it was a prime piece of real estate. The fact that he'd have to raze it to the ground to build a hotel on it was just par for the course.

Of course his kid brother wouldn't understand that, and he wasn't in the mood to explain it. He'd left Mexico when Ricardo had been young. Ricardo had cried. Cruz had not. Surprisingly, after he'd returned home with his tail between his legs eight years ago, he and his brother had picked up from where they'd left off, their bond intact. It was the only bond that was.

'I'm fine.' He swung his gaze to Lauren. 'And I'm not concerned about Aspen Carmichael. Old man Carmichael died owing more money than he had, thanks to the GFC, so there's no way she can have that sort of cash lying around.'

'No, she doesn't,' Lauren agreed. 'She's borrowing it.'

Cruz stilled. Now, that was just plain stupid. He knew Ocean Haven agisted horses and raised good-quality polo ponies, but no way would either of those bring in the type of money they were talking about.

'She'll never get it.'

Lauren looked as if she knew better. 'My sources tell me she's actually pretty close.'

Cruz ignored Ricardo's interested gaze and kept his face visibly relaxed. 'How close?'

'Two-thirds close.'

'Twenty million! Who would be stupid enough to lend her twenty million US dollars in this economic climate?' And, more importantly, what was she using for collateral?

Lauren raised her eyebrows at his uncharacteristic outburst, but wisely stayed silent.

'Hell!' The burst of adrenaline he used to feel when he mounted one of his ponies before a major event winged through his blood. How on earth had she managed to raise that much money and what could he do about it?

'Do you want me to start negotiating with her?' Lauren queried.

'No.' He turned his ordinarily agile mind to come up with a solution, but all it produced was an image of a radiant teenager decked out in figure-hugging jodhpurs and a fitted shirt leaning against a white fencepost, laughing and chatting while the sun turned her wheat-blonde curls to gold. His jaw clenched and his body hardened. Great. A hard-on in gym shorts. 'You focus on Joe Carmichael and any other offers lurking in the wings,' he instructed his lawyer. 'I'll handle Aspen Carmichael.'

'Of course,' Lauren concurred with a brief smile.

'In the meantime find out who Aspen is borrowing from and what exactly she's offering as collateral—' although as to that he had his ideas '—and meet me in my Acapulco office in an hour.'

Ricardo waited until Lauren had disappeared before tossing the rubber ball into the air. 'You didn't tell me you were buying the Carmichael place.'

'Why would I? It's just business.'

Ricardo's eyebrows lifted. 'And *handling* the lovely Aspen Carmichael will be part of that business?'

People said Cruz had a certain look that he got just before a major event which told his opponents they might as well pack up and go home. He gave it to his brother now. 'This is not your concern.'

His brother, unfortunately, was one of the few people who ignored it.

'Maybe not, but you once swore you'd never set foot on Ocean Haven again. So, what gives?'

What gave, Cruz thought, was that old Charlie had kicked the bucket and his son, Aspen's uncle, Joseph Carmichael, couldn't afford to run the estate and keep his English bride in diamonds and champagne so was moving to England. Cruz had assumed Aspen would be going with them—to sponge off him now that her grandfather was out of the picture.

It seemed he had assumed wrong.

But he had no intention of talking about his plans with his overly sentimental brother, who would no doubt assume there was more to it than a simple opportunity to make a lot of money. 'I don't have time to talk about it now,' he said, making a split-second decision. 'I need to organise the jet.'

'You're flying to East Hampton?'

'And if I am?' Cruz growled.

Ricardo held his hands up as if he was placating an angry bear. 'Miama's surprise birthday party is tomorrow.'

Cruz strode towards the changing rooms, his mind already in Hampton—or more specifically in Ocean Haven. 'Don't count on me being there.'

'Given your track record, the only person who still has enough hope to do that is Miama herself.'

Cruz stopped. Ricardo's blunt words stabbed him in the heart. His family still meant everything to him, and he'd help any of them out in a heartbeat, but things just weren't the same any more. With the exception of Ricardo, none of his family knew how to treat him, and his mother constantly threw him guilty looks that were a persistent reminder of the darker days of his youth after he'd gone to the farm.

Charles Carmichael had been a difficult man with a formidable temper who'd liked to get his own way, and Cruz had never been one to back down from a fight until *that* night. No, it had not been an easy transition for a proud thirteen-year-old to make, and if there was one thing Cruz hated more than the capricious nature of the human race it was dwelling on the past.

He glanced back at Ricardo. 'You're going to be stubborn about this, aren't you?'

Ricardo laughed. 'You've cornered the market in stubborn, *mi amigo*. I'm just persistent.'

'Persistently painful. You know, bro, you don't need a wife. You *are* a wife.'

Aspen decided that she had a new-found respect for telemarketers. It wasn't easy being told no time after time and then picking yourself up and continuing on. But like anyone trying to make a living she had to toughen up and stay positive. Stay on track. Especially when she was so close to achieving her goal. To choke now or, worse, give up, would mean failing in her attempt to keep her beloved home and that was inconceivable.

Smiling up at the beef of a man in front of her as if she didn't have a head full of doubts and fears, Aspen surreptitiously pulled at the waist of the silk dress she'd worn to impress the polo patrons attending the midweek chukkas they held at Ocean Haven throughout the summer months.

In the searing sunshine the dress had taken on the texture of a wet dishrag and it did little to improve her mood as she listened to Billy Smyth the Third, son of one of her late grandfather's arch enemies, wax lyrical about the game of polo he had—thankfully—just won.

'Oh, yes,' she murmured. 'I heard it was the goal of

the afternoon.' Fed to him, she had no doubt, by his well-paid polo star, who knew very well which side his bread was buttered on.

Billy Smyth was a rich waste of space who sponged off his father's cardboard packaging empire and loved every minute of it—not unlike many others in their circle. Her ex-husband still continued unashamedly to live off his own family's wealth, but thankfully he'd been out of her life for a long time, and she wasn't going to ruin an already difficult day by thinking about him as well.

Instead she concentrated on the wealthy man in front of her, with his polished boots and his pot belly propped over the top of his starchy white polo jeans. Years ago she had tried to like Billy, but he was very much a part of the 'women should keep silent and look beautiful' brigade, and the fact that she was pandering to his unhealthy ego at all was testament to just how desperate she had become.

When he'd asked her to meet him after the game she had jumped at the chance, knowing she'd dance on the sun in a bear suit if it would mean he'd lend her the last ten million she needed to keep Ocean Haven. Though by the gleam in his eyes he'd probably want her naked—and she wasn't so desperate that she'd actually hawk herself.

Yet.

Ever, she amended.

So she continued to smile and present her plan to turn 'The Farm', as Ocean Haven was lovingly referred to, into a viable commercial entity that any savvy businessman would feel remiss for not investing in. So far two of her grandfather's old friends had come on board, but she was fast feeling as if she was running out of options to find the rest. Ten million was small change to Billy and, she thought, ignoring the way his eyes made her skin crawl as if she was covered in live ants, he seemed genuinely interested.

'Your grandpop would be rolling in his grave at the thought of the Smyths investing in The Farm,' he announced.

True—but only because her grandfather had been an unforgiving, hard-headed traditionalist. 'He's not here anymore.' Aspen reminded him. 'And without the money Uncle Joe is going to sell to the highest bidder.'

Billy cocked his head and considered his way slowly down to her feet and just as slowly back up. 'Word is he already has a winner.'

Aspen took a minute to relax her shoulders, telling herself that Billy really didn't mean to be offensive. 'Yes. Some super-rich consortium that will no doubt want to put a hotel on it. But I'm determined to keep The Farm in the family. I'm sure you understand how important that is, being such a devoted family man yourself.'

A slow smile crept over Billy's face and Aspen inwardly groaned. She was trying too hard and they both knew it.

'Yes, indeed I do.'

Billy leered. His smile grew wider. And when he rocked back on his heels Aspen sent up a silent prayer to save her from having to deal with arrogant men ever again.

Because that was exactly why she was in this situation in the first place. Her grandfather had believed in three things: testosterone, power, and tradition. In other words men should inherit the earth while women should be grateful that they had. And he had used his fearsome iron will to control everyone who dared to disagree with him.

When her mother had died suddenly just before Aspen's tenth birthday and—surprise surprise—her errant father couldn't be located, Aspen had been sent to live with her grandfather and her uncle. Her grandmother had passed away a long time before. Aspen had liked Uncle Joe immediately, but he'd never been much of an advocate for her during her grandfather's attempts to turn her into the perfect debutante.

So far she had been at the mercy of her controlling grandfather, then her controlling ex, and now her misguided, henpecked uncle.

'I'm sorry Aspen,' her Uncle Joe had said when she'd managed to pin him down in the library a month ago. 'Father left the property in my hands to do with as I saw fit.'

'Yes, but he wouldn't have expected you to *sell it*,' Aspen had beseeched him.

'He shouldn't have expected Joe to sort out the mess of his finances either,' Joe's determined wife Tammy had whined.

'He wasn't well these last few years.' Aspen had appealed to her aunt, but, knowing that wouldn't do any good, had turned back to her uncle. 'Don't sell Ocean Haven, Uncle Joe. Please. It's been in our family for one hundred and fifty years. Your blood is in this land.'

Her mother's heart was here in this land.

But her uncle had shaken his head. 'I'm sorry, Aspen, I need the money. But unlike Father I'm not a greedy man. If you can raise the price I need in time for my Russian investment, with a little left over for the house Tammy wants in Knightsbridge, then you can have Ocean Haven and all the problems that go with it.'

'*What?*'

'*What?*'

Aspen and her Aunt Tammy had cried in unison.

'Joseph Carmichael, that is preposterous,' Tammy had said.

But for once Uncle Joe had stood up to his wife. 'I'd always planned to provide for Aspen, so this is a way to do it. But I think you're crazy for wanting to keep this place.' He'd shaken his head at her.

Aspen had been so happy she had all but floated out of

the room. Then reality at what exactly her uncle had offered had set in and she'd got the shakes. It was an enormous amount of money to pay back but she *knew* if she got the chance she could do it.

The horn signifying the end of the last chukka blew and Aspen pushed aside her fear that maybe she *was* just a little crazy.

'Listen, Billy, it's a great deal,' she snapped, forgetting all about the proper manners her grandfather had drummed into her as a child, and also forgetting that Billy was probably her last great hope of controlling her own future. 'Take it or leave it.'

Oh, yes and losing that firecracker temper of yours is sure to sway him, she berated herself.

A tiny dust cloud rose between them as Billy made a figure eight with his boots in the dirt. 'The thing is, Aspen, we're busy enough over at Oaks Place, and even though you've done a good job of hiding it The Farm needs a lot of work.'

'It needs some,' Aspen agreed with forced calm, thinking she hadn't done a good job at all if he'd seen through her patchwork maintenance attempts. 'But I've factored all that into the plan.' *Sort of.*

'I just think I need a bit more of a persuasive argument if I'm to take this to my daddy,' he suggested, a certain look crossing his pampered face.

'Like…?' A tight band had formed around Aspen's chest because, really, it was hard to miss what he meant.

'Well, hell, Aspen, you're not that naïve. You *have* been married.'

Yes, unfortunately she had. But all that had done was make her determined that she would never be at any man's mercy again. Which was exactly where arrogant, controlling men like this one wanted their women to be. 'For just you, Billy?' she simpered. 'Or for your daddy as well?'

It took Mr Cocksure a second or two to realise she was yanking his chain and when he did his big head reared back and his eyes narrowed. 'I ain't no pimp, lady.'

'No,' she said calmly, flicking her riot of honey-coloured spiral curls back over her shoulder. 'What you are is a dirty, rotten rat and I can see why Grandpa Charles said your kind were just slime.' *Who gave a damn about proper manners anyway?*

Instead of getting angry Billy threw back his head and hooted with laughter. 'You know. I can't believe the rumours that you're a cold one in the sack. Not with all that fire shooting out of those pretty green eyes of yours.' He reached out and ran a finger down the side of her cheek and grinned when she raised her hand to rub at it. 'Let me know when you change your mind. I like a woman with attitude.'

Before she could open her mouth to tell him she'd mention that to his wife he sauntered off, leaving her spitting mad. She watched him pick up a glass of champagne from a table before joining a group of sweaty riders and willed someone to grab it and throw it all over him.

Of course no one did. Fate wasn't that kind.

Turning away in disgust, she cursed under her breath when a gust of hot wind whipped her hair across her face. Too angry to stop and clear her vision, she would have walked straight into a wall if it hadn't reached out and grabbed her by her upper arms.

With a soft gasp she looked up, about to thank whoever had saved her. But the words never came and the quick smile froze on her face as she found herself staring into the hard eyes of a man she had thought she would never see in the flesh again.

The air between them split apart and reformed, vibrating with emotion as Cruz Rodriquez stared down at her with such cold detachment she nearly shivered.

Eight years dissolved into dust. Guilt, shame and a host of other emotions all sparked for dominance inside her.

'I...' Aspen blinked, her mind scrambling for poise... words...*something.*

'Hello, Aspen. Nice to see you again.'

Aspen blinked at the incongruity of those words. He might as well have said *Off with her head.*

'I...'

CHAPTER TWO

CRUZ STARED DOWN at the slender woman whose smooth arms he held and wished he hadn't left his sunglasses in the car. At seventeen Aspen Carmichael had been full of sexual promise. Eight years later, with her golden mane flowing down past her shoulders and the top button of her dress artfully popped open to reveal the upper swell of her creamy assets, she had well and truly delivered. And he was finding it hard not to take her all in at once.

'You…?' he prompted casually, dropping his hands and raising his eyes from her cleavage.

She glanced down and quickly closed the top of her dress. Clearly only men offering part of their vast fortunes were allowed to view the merchandise. The realisation of his earlier assumption as to what she might be using as leverage to raise her cash was for some reason profoundly disappointing.

'I…' She shook her head as if to clear it. 'What are you doing here?'

'Old Charlie would roll over in his grave if he heard you greeting a polo patron like that,' Cruz drawled. *Even one he didn't think would ever be good enough for his perfect little granddaughter,* he added silently.

Cruz's velveteen voice, with no hint at all of his Mexican heritage, scraped over Aspen's already raw nerves and she didn't manage to contain the shiver this time.

She couldn't tell his frame of mind but she knew hers and it was definitely disturbed. 'My grandfather probably feels like he's on a spit roast at the moment.' She smiled, trying for light amusement to ease the tension that lay as thick as the issues of the past between them.

'Are you implying he's in hell, Aspen?'

He probably was, Aspen thought, but that wasn't what she'd meant. 'No. I just…you're right.' She shook her head, wondering what had happened to her manners. Her composure. Her *brain*. 'That was a terrible greeting. Shall we start again?'

Without waiting for him to reply she stuck out her hand, ignoring the racing memories causing her heart to beat double time.

'Hello, Cruz, welcome back to Ocean Haven. You're looking well.' Which was a half-truth if ever she'd uttered one.

The man didn't look well. He looked superb.

His thick black hair that sat just fashionably shy of his expensive suit jacket and his piercing black eyes and square-cut jaw were even more beautiful than she remembered. He'd always had a strong, angular face and powerful body, but eight years had done him a load of favours in the looks department, settling a handsome maturity over the youthful virility he'd always worn like a cloak.

The apology she'd never got to voice for her part in the acrimonious accusations that had no doubt contributed to him leaving Ocean Haven eight years ago hovered behind her closed lips, but it seemed awkward to just blurt it out.

How could she tell him that a couple of months after that night she had written him a letter explaining everything but hadn't had the wherewithal to send it without feeling a deep sense of shame at her ineptitude? It was little comfort knowing she'd been distracted by her grandfather's stroke at the time, because she knew her behaviour that night had

probably brought that on too. After he had recovered sending Cruz a letter had seemed like too little too late, and
she'd pushed out of her mind the man who had fascinated
her during most of her teenage years.

And maybe he was here now to let bygones be bygones.
She didn't know, but why pre-empt anything with her own
guilt-riddled memories?

Because it would make you feel better, that's why.

'As are you.'

As she was what? Oh, looking well. 'Thank you.' She
ran a nervous hand down the side of her dress and then
pretended she was flicking off horse dust. 'So…ah…are
you here for the polo? The last chukka just finished, but—'

'I'm not here for the polo.'

Aspen hated the anxious feeling that had settled over
her and raised her chin. 'Well, there's champagne in the
central marquee. Just tell Judy that I sent—'

'I'm not here for the champagne either.'

Even more perturbed by the way he regarded her with
such cool detachment she felt as if she was frying under
the blasted summer sun. 'Well, it would be great if you
could tell me what you *are* here for because I have a few
more people to schmooze before they leave. You know
how these things go.'

He looked at her as if he was seeing right inside her.
As if he knew all her secrets. As if he could see how desperately uncomfortable she was. *Impossible*, she thought,
telling herself to get a grip.

Cruz could almost see the sweat breaking out over Aspen's body and noted the way her cat-green eyes wouldn't
quite meet his. He didn't know if that was because he
was keeping her from an assignation with Billy Smyth,
or someone else, or because she could feel the chemistry
that lay between them like a grenade with the pin pulled.

Whatever it was, she wasn't leaving his side until he

had won over her confidence and figured out a way to handle the situation.

His brother's silky question about 'handling the lovely Aspen Carmichael' came into his head. He knew what Ricardo had meant and looking at Aspen now, in her svelte designer dress and 'come take me' heels, her wild hair curling down around her shoulders as if she'd just rolled out of her latest lover's bed, he had no doubt many men had 'handled' her that way before. But not him. Never him.

So far he'd drawn a blank as to how to contain her money-grabbing endeavours without alerting her to his own interest in Ocean Haven. Until he did he'd just have to rein himself in and keep his eyes away from her sexy mouth.

'I'm here to buy a horse, Aspen. What else?'

'A horse?'

Aspen blinked. That was the last thing she had expected him to say, though what she *had* expected she couldn't say.

'You do have one for sale, don't you?' he continued silkily.

Aspen cleared her throat. 'Gypsy Blue. She's a thoroughbred. Ex-racing stock and she's gorgeous.'

'I have no doubt.'

Aspen frowned at his tone, wondering why he seemed so tense. Not that he *looked* tense. In his bespoke suit with his hands in his pockets, his hair casually ruffled by the warm breeze, he looked like a man who didn't have a care in the world. But the vibe she was picking up from him was making her feel edgy—and surely that wasn't just because of her sense of guilt.

'Are you hoping the horse will materialise in front of us, Aspen, or are you going to take me to see her?'

'I…' Aspen felt stupid, and not a little perturbed to be standing there trying not to look at his chiselled mouth. Which was nearly impossible when the memory of the kiss they had shared on that awful night was swirling inside her head. 'Of course.' She glanced around, hoping to see Donny, but knew that was cowardly. It was really *her* responsibility to show him the mare, not her chief groom's.

'She played earlier today, so she should be in the south stables.' It was just rotten luck that she happened to be in the building where she had kissed Cruz on that fateful night. 'Hey, why don't I take you past the east paddock?' she said, using anything as a possible distraction. 'Trigger is out there, and I know he'd remember you and—'

'I'm not here on a social visit, Aspen.'

And don't mistake it for one, his tone implied.

No polo, no champagne, no socialising. Got it.

Still, she hesitated at his sharp tone. Then decided to let it drop and listened to the sound of their feet crunching the gravel as they walked away from the busy sounds of horse-owners loading tired horses into their respective trucks. It was all very normal and busy at the end of the afternoon's practice, and yet Aspen felt as if she was wading through quicksand with Cruz beside her.

She cast a curious glance at him and wondered if he felt the same way. Or maybe he didn't feel anything at all and just wanted to do his business and head out like everyone else. In a way she hoped that was the case, because the shock of seeing him again had worn off and his tension was raising her stress levels to dangerous proportions.

But then he had a reason for being tense, she reminded herself, and her skin flushed hotly as the weight of the past bore down on her. Years ago she had promised herself that she would never let pride interfere with the decisions she made in her life, but in avoiding the elephant walking alongside them wasn't that exactly what she was doing now?

Taking a deep breath, she stopped just short of the stable

doors and turned to Cruz, determined to rectify the situation as best she could *before* they made it inside.

Shading her eyes with one hand, she looked up into his face. Had he always been this tall? This broad? This good-looking?

'Cruz, listen. This feels really awkward, but you took me by surprise before when I ran into you—*literally*.' She released a shaky breath. 'I want you to know that I feel terrible about the way you left The Farm all those years ago, and I'm truly sorry for the role I played in that.'

'Are you?' he asked coolly.

'Yes, of course. I never meant for you to get into trouble.'

Cruz didn't move a muscle.

'I didn't!' Aspen felt her temper flare at his dubious look, hating how defensive she sounded.

She'd gone down to the stables that night because Chad—now thankfully her ex—had stayed for dinner so he could present his idea to her grandfather that he would marry her as soon as she turned eighteen. Aspen remembered how overwhelmed she had felt when neither man would consider her desire to study before she even thought about the prospect of marriage.

She'd known it was what her grandfather wanted, and at the time pleasing him had been more important than pleasing herself. So she'd done what she'd always done when she was stressed and gone down to be with the horses and to reconnect with her mother in her special place in the main stable.

Gone to try and make sense of her feelings.

Of course in hindsight letting her frustration get to her and kicking the side of the stable wall in steel-capped boots hadn't been all that clever, because it had brought Cruz down from his apartment over the garage to investigate.

She remembered that he had looked gorgeous and lean

and bad in dirty jeans and a half-buttoned shirt, as if he had just climbed out of bed.

'What's got you in a snit, *chiquita*?' he'd said, the intensity of his heavy-lidded gaze in the dim light belying the relaxed humour in his voice.

'Wouldn't you like to know?' she'd thrown back at him challengingly.

Inwardly grimacing, she remembered how she had flicked her hair back over her shoulder in an unconscious gesture to get his full attention. She hadn't known what she was inviting—not really—but she hadn't wanted him to go. For some reason she had remembered the time she had come across him kissing a girlfriend in the outer barn, and the soft, pleasure-filled moans the girl had made had filled her ears that night.

Acting purely on instinct she had wandered from horse stall to horse stall, eventually coming to a stop directly in front of him. The warm glow of his torch had seemed to make the world contract, so that it had felt as if they were the only two people in it. Aspen was pretty sure she'd reached for him first, but seconds later she had been bent over his arm and he had been kissing her.

Her first kiss.

She felt her breathing grow shallow at the memory.

Something had fired in her system that night—desperation, lust, need—whatever it had been she'd never felt anything like it before or since.

Looking back, it was obvious that a feeling of entrapment—a feeling of having no say over her future—had driven her into the stables that night, but it had been Cruz's sheer animal magnetism that had driven her into his arms.

Not that she really wanted to admit any of that to him right now. Not when he looked so...*bored*.

'This is old news, Aspen, and I'm not in the mood to reminisce.'

'That's your prerogative. But I want you to know that I told my grandfather the next day that he'd got it wrong.'

'Really?'

'Yes, really.' But her grandfather had cut her off with a look of disgust she hadn't wanted to face. She looked up at Cruz now, more sorry than she could say. 'I'm—'

'Truly sorry? So you said. Have you become prone to repeating yourself?'

Aspen blinked up at him. Was it her imagination or did he hate her? 'No, but I don't think you believe me,' she said carefully.

'Does it matter if I do?'

'Well, we used to be friends.'

'We were never *friends*, Aspen. But I was glad to see your little indiscretion didn't stop Anderson from marrying you.'

Aspen moistened her parched lips. 'Grandfather thought it best if I didn't tell him.'

Cruz barked out a laugh. 'Well, now I almost feel sorry for the fool. If he'd known what a disloyal little cheat you were from the start he might have saved himself the heartache at the end.'

Oh, yes, he hated her all right. 'Look, I'm sorry I brought it up. I just wanted to clear the air between us.'

'There's nothing to clear as far as I'm concerned.'

Aspen studied him warily. He wasn't moving but she felt as if she was being circled by a predator. A very angry predator. She didn't believe that he was at all okay with what had transpired between them but who was she to push it?

'I made a mistake, but as you said you're not here to reminisce.' And nor was she. Particularly not about a time in her life she would much rather forget had ever happened.

She turned sharply towards the stables and kept up a brisk pace until she reached the doors, only starting to feel herself relax as she entered the cooler interior, her high heels clicking loudly on the bluestone floor. Her nose was filled with the sweet scent of horse and hay.

Cruz followed and Aspen glanced around at the worn tack hanging from metal bars and the various frayed blankets and dirty buckets that waited for Donny and her to come and finish them off for the day. The high beams of the hayloft needed a fresh coat of paint, and if you looked closely there were tiny pinpricks of sunlight streaming in through the tin roof where there shouldn't be. She hoped Cruz didn't look up.

A pigeon created dust motes as it swooped past them and interested horses poked their noses over the stall doors. A couple whinnied when they recognised her.

Aspen automatically reached into her pocket for a treat, forgetting that she wasn't in her normal jeans and shirt. Instead she brushed one of the horses' noses. 'Sorry, hon. I don't have anything. I'll bring you something later.'

Cruz stopped beside her but he didn't try to stroke the horse as she remembered he might once have done.

'This is Cougar. Named because he has the heart of a mountain lion, although he can be a bit sulky when he gets pushed around out on the field. Can't you, big guy?' She gave him an affectionate pat before moving to the next stall. 'This one is Delta. She's—'

'Just show me the horse you're selling, Aspen.'

Aspen read the flash of annoyance in his gaze—and something else she couldn't place. But his annoyance fed hers and once again she stalked away from him and stopped at Gypsy Blue's stall. If she'd been able to afford it she would have kept her beloved mare, and that only increased her aggravation.

'Here she is,' she rapped out. 'Her sire was Blue Rise, her dam Lady Belington. You might remember she won the Kentucky Derby twice running a few years back.' She sucked in a breath, trying not to babble as she had done over her apology before. If Cruz was happy with the way things were between them then so was she. 'I have someone else interested, so if you want her you'll have to decide quickly.'

Quite a backpedal, Cruz thought. From uncomfortable, apologetic innocent to stiff Upper East Side princess. He wondered what other roles she had up her sleeve and then cut the thought in half before it could fully form. Because he already knew, didn't he? Cheating temptress being one of them. Not that she was married now. Or engaged as far as he knew.

'I've made you angry,' he said, backpedalling himself.

This wasn't at all the way he needed her to be if he was going to get information out of her. It was just this damned place. It felt as if it was full of ghosts, with memories around every corner that he had no wish to revisit. He'd closed the door on that part of his life the minute he'd carried his duffel bag off the property. On foot. Taking nothing from Old Man Carmichael except the clothes on his back and the money he'd already earned.

Of its own accord his gaze shifted to the other end of the long walkway to the place where Aspen had approached him that night, wearing a cotton nightie she must have known was see-through in the glow of his torch. He hadn't been wearing much either, having only thrown on a pair of jeans and a shirt he hadn't even bothered to button properly when he'd heard something banging on the wall and gone to investigate.

He'd presumed it was one of the horses and had been absolutely thunderstruck to find Aspen in that nightie and a pair of riding boots. She'd looked hotter than Hades and when she'd strolled past the stalls, lightly trailing her slender fingers along the wood, he couldn't have moved if someone had planted a bomb under him.

It had all been a ploy. He knew that now. He'd kissed her because he'd been a man overcome with lust. She'd kissed him because she'd been setting him up. It had been like a bad rendition of Samson and Delilah and she'd deserved an acting award for wardrobe choice alone.

His muscles grew taut as he remembered how he had held himself in check. How he hadn't wanted to overwhelm her with the desperate hunger that had surged through him and urged him to pull her down onto the hay and rip the flimsy nightie from her body. How he hadn't wanted to take her *innocence*. What a joke. She'd played him like a finely tuned instrument and, like a fool, he'd let her.

'Like I said before.' She cleared her throat. 'This feels a little awkward.'

She must have noticed the direction of his gaze because her voice sounded breathless; almost as if her memories of that night mirrored his own. Of course he knew better now.

About to placate her by pretending he had forgotten all about it, he found the words dying in his throat as she raised both hands and twisted her flyaway curls into a rope and let it drop down her back. The middle button on her dress strained and he found himself willing it to pop open.

Surprised to find his libido running away without his consent, he quickly ducked inside the stall and feigned avid interest in a horse he had no wish to buy.

He went through the motions, though, studying the lines of the mare's back, running his hands over her glossy coat, stroking down over her foreleg and checking the straightness of her pasterns. Fortunately he was on auto-pilot, because his undisciplined mind was comparing the shapeliness of the thoroughbred with Aspen's lissom figure and imagining how she would feel under his rough hands.

Silky, smooth, and oh, so soft.

Memories of the little sounds she'd made as he'd lost

himself in her eight years ago exploded through his system and turned his breathing rough.

'She's an exceptional polo pony. Really relaxed on the field and fast as a whip.'

Aspen's commentary dragged his mind back to his game plan and he kept on stroking the horse as he spoke. 'Why are you selling her?'

'We run a horse stud, not a bed and breakfast,' she said with mock sternness, her eyes tinged with dark humour as she repeated one of Charles Carmichael's favourite sayings.

'Or an old persons' home.' He joined in with Charles's second favourite saying before he could stop himself.

'No.' Her small smile was tinged with emotion.

Her reaction surprised him.

'You miss him?'

She shifted and leant her elbows on the door. 'I really don't know.' Her eyes trailed over the horse. 'He had moments of such kindness, and he gave me a home when Mum died, but he was impossible to be around if he didn't get his own way.'

'He certainly had high hopes of you marrying well and providing blue stock heirs for Ocean Haven.' And he'd made it more than clear to him after Aspen had returned to the house that night that Cruz wouldn't be the one to provide them under any circumstances.

'Yes.'

Her troubled eyes briefly met his and for a moment he wanted to shake her for not being a different kind of woman. A more sincere and genuine woman.

'So what do you think?'

It took him a minute to realise she was talking about the mare and not herself. 'She's perfect. I'll take her.'

'Oh.' She gave a self-conscious laugh. 'You don't want to ride her first?'

Oh, yes, he certainly did want to do that!
'No.'

'Well, I did tell you to be quick. I'll have Donny run the paperwork.'

'Send it to my lawyer.' Cruz rubbed the mare's nose and let her nudge him. 'I hear Joe is planning to sell the farm.'

She grimaced. 'Good news travels fast.'

'Polo's a small community.'

'Too small sometimes.' She gestured towards the mare. 'She'll ruin your nice suit if you let her do that.'

'I have others.'

So nice not to have to worry about money, Aspen thought, a touch enviously. After the abject poverty she and her mother had lived in after her father's desertion, the wealth of Ocean Haven had been staggering. It was something she'd never take for granted again.

'Where are you planning to go once it's sold?'

'It's not going to be sold,' she said with a touch of asperity, stepping back as Cruz joined her outside the stall. 'At least not to someone else.'

He raised an eyebrow. 'You're going to buy it?'

'Yes.' She had always been a believer in the power of positive thinking, and she had never needed that more than she did now.

Gypsy Blue whickered and stuck her head over the door and Aspen realised her water trough was nearly empty. Unhooking it, she walked the short distance to a tap and filled it.

'Let me do that.'

Cruz took the bucket from her before she could stop him and stepped inside the stall. Aspen grabbed the feed bucket Donny had left outside and followed him in and hooked it into place.

'It's a big property to run by yourself,' he said.

'For a girl?' she replied curtly.

'I didn't say that.'

'Sorry. I'm a bit touchy because so many people have implied more than once that I won't be able to do it. It's like they think I'm completely incompetent, and that really gets my—' She gave a small laugh realising she was about to unload her biggest gripe onto him and he was virtually a stranger to her now. Why would he even care? 'The fact is…' She looked at him carefully.

He had money. She'd heard of his business acumen. Of the companies he bought and sold. Of his innovative and brilliant new polo-inspired hotel in Mexico. He was the epitome of a man at the top of his game. Right now, as he leant his wide shoulders against the stall door and blocked out all sources of light from behind, he also looked the epitome of adult male perfection.

'But the fact is…?' he prompted.

Aspen's eyes darted to his as she registered the subtle amusement lacing his voice. Did he know what she had just been thinking? 'Sorry, I was just…' *Just a bit distracted by your incredible face? Your powerful body? Way to go, Aspen. Really. Super effort.* 'The fact is—' she squared her shoulders '—I need ten million dollars to keep it.'

She forced a bright smile onto her face.

'You're not looking for an investment opportunity, are you?'

CHAPTER THREE

SHE COULDN'T BELIEVE she'd actually voiced the question that had just formed in her mind but she knew that she had when Cruz's dark gaze sharpened on hers. But frankly, with only five days left to raise the rest of the money and Billy Smyth firmly out of the picture, she really was that desperate.

'Give you ten million dollars? That's a big ask.'

Her heart thumped loudly in her chest and her mouth felt dust dry. 'Lend,' she corrected. 'But you know what they say…' She stopped as he straightened to his full height and she lost her train of thought.

He shoved both hands into his pockets. '*They* say a lot of things, Aspen. What is it exactly you're referring to?'

'If you don't ask you never know,' she said, moistening her lips. 'And I'm desperate.'

Cruz's eyes glittered as he looked down at her. 'A good negotiator never shows that particular hand. It puts their opponent in the dominant position.'

Heat bloomed anew on her face as his tone seemed to take on a sensual edge. 'I don't see you as my opponent, Cruz.'

'Then you're a fool,' he returned, almost too mildly.

Aspen felt her hopes shrivel to nothing. What had she been thinking, approaching a business situation like that? Where was her professionalism? Her polish?

But maybe she'd known he'd never agree to it. Not with the way he obviously felt about her.

'What would I get out of it, anyway?'

The unexpected question surprised her and once again her eyes darted to his. Had she been wrong in thinking he wouldn't be interested? 'A lot, actually. I've drawn up a business plan.'

'Really?'

She didn't like his sceptical tone but decided to ignore it. 'Yes. It outlines the horses due to foal, and how much we expect to make from each one, and our plans to purchase a top-of-the-line stallion to keep improving the breed. We also have a couple of wonderful horses we're about to start training—and I don't know if you've heard of our riding school, but I teach adults and children, and—well… There's more, but if you're truly interested we can run through the logistics of it all later.' Out of breath, she stopped, and then added, 'It has merit. I promise.'

'If it has so much merit why haven't any of the financial institutions bankrolled you?'

'Because I'm young—that is usually the first excuse. But really I think it's because unbeknownst to any of us Grandfather hadn't been running his business properly the last few years and—' Realising that yet again she was about to divulge every one of her issues, she stopped. 'The banks just don't believe I have enough experience to pull it off.'

'Perhaps you should have thought about furthering your education instead of marrying to secure your future.'

Aspen nearly gasped at his snide tone of voice. 'I didn't marry to secure anything,' she said sharply. Except perhaps her grandfather's love and affection. Something that had always been in short supply.

Upset with herself for even being in this position, and with him for his nasty comment, Aspen thought about telling him that she was one semester out from completing a degree in veterinary science—and that she'd achieved that while working full-time running Ocean Haven. But she knew that in her current state she would no doubt come across as defensive or whiney, and that only made her angry.

'If you have such a low opinion of me why pretend any interest in my plans for The Farm?' she demanded hotly, slapping her hands either side of her waist. 'Are you planning to steal our ideas?'

That got an abrupt bark of laughter from him that did nothing to improve her temper. 'I don't need to steal your ideas, *gatita*. I have plenty of my own.'

'Then why get my hopes up like that?'

'Is that what I did?'

Aspen stared him down. 'You know that's exactly what you did.'

He stepped closer to her. 'But maybe I *am* interested.'

His tone sent a splinter of unease down her spine but she was too annoyed to pay attention to it. 'Don't patronise me, Cruz. I have five days before The Farm will be sold to some big-shot investment consortium. I don't have time to bandy around with this.'

'Ocean Haven really means that much to you?'

'Yes, it does.'

'I suppose it *is* the easiest option for a woman in your position,' he conceded, with such arrogance that Aspen nearly choked.

Easy? Easy! He clearly had no idea how hard she worked on the property—tending horses, mending fences, keeping the books—nor how important Ocean Haven was to her. How it was the one link she had left with her mother. How it was the one place that had made her feel happy and secure after she'd been orphaned. After her marriage had fallen apart.

She was incredibly proud of her work and her future plans to open up a school camp for kids who'd had a tough start in life. Horses had a way of grounding troubled adolescents and she wanted to provide a place they could come to and feel safe. Just as she had. And she hated that Cruz was judging her—*mocking her*—like every other obnoxious male she had ever come across. That she hadn't expected it from him only made her feel worse.

Hopping mad, she had a mind to order him off her property, but she couldn't quite kill off this avenue of hope just yet. He was supposed to be a savvy businessman after all, and she had a good plan. Well, she hoped she did. 'Ocean Haven has been in my family for centuries,' she began, striving for calm.

'I think the violinist has packed up for the day…'

Aspen blinked. 'God, you're cold. I don't remember that about you.'

'Don't you, *gatita*? Tell me…'

His voice dropped an octave and her heartbeat faltered. 'What *do* you remember?'

Aspen's gaze fell to his mouth. 'I remember that you were…' *Tall. That your hair glints almost blue-black in the sun. That your face looks like it belongs in a magazine. That your mouth is firm and yet soft.* She forced her eyes to meet his and ignored the fact that her face felt as if it was on fire. 'Good with the horses.' She swallowed. 'That you were smart, and that you used to keep to yourself a lot. But I remember when you laughed.' *It used to make me smile.* 'It sounded happy. And I remember that when you were mad at something not even my grandfather was brave enough to face you. I rem—'

'Enough.' He sliced his hand through the air with sharp finality. 'There's only one thing I want to know right now,' he said softly.

If she remembered his kisses? Yes—yes, she did. Sometimes even when she didn't want to. 'What?' she asked, hating the breathless quality of her voice.

'Just how desperate *are* you?'

His dark voice was so dangerously male it sent her brain into overdrive. 'What kind of a question is that?' She shook her head, trying to ward off the jittery feelings he so effortlessly conjured up inside her.

He reached forward and captured a strand of her hair between his fingertips, his eyes burning into hers. 'If I were to lend you this money I'd want more than a share in the profits.'

Aspen felt her chest rising and falling too quickly and hoped to hell he wasn't going to suggest the very thing Billy Smyth had done not an hour earlier.

Reaching up, she tugged her hair out of his hold. 'Such as...?'

His eyes looked black as pitch as they pinned her like a dart on a wall. 'Oh, save us both the Victorian naïveté. You're no retiring virgin after the life you lived with Chad Anderson—and before that, even. You're a sensual woman who no doubt looks very good gracing a man's bed.' He paused, his gaze caressing her face. 'If the terms were right I might want you to grace mine.'

Was he kidding?

Aspen felt her mouth drop open before she could stop it. Rage welled up inside her like a living beast. Rage at the injustice of her grandfather's will, rage at the way men viewed her as little more than a sexual object, rage at her mother's death and her father's abandonment.

Maybe Cruz had a reason for being upset with her after she had failed to correct her grandfather's assumption that they were sleeping together years ago, but that didn't give him the right to treat her like a—like a whore.

'Get out of my way,' she ordered.

His eyes lingered on her tight lips. 'Make sure you don't

burn your bridges unnecessarily, Aspen. Pride can be a nasty thing when it's used rashly.'

She knew all about pride going before a fall. 'It's not rash pride making me reject your offer, Cruz. It's simple self-respect.'

'Whatever you want to call it, I'm offering you a straightforward business deal. You have something I've decided I want. I have something you need. Why complicate it?'

'Because it's disgusting.'

'What an interesting way to put it,' he sneered. 'Tell me, Aspen, would it have been less *disgusting* if I'd first said that you were beautiful before taking you to bed? If I'd first invited you out for a drink? Taken you to dinner, perhaps?' He took a step towards her and lowered his voice. 'If I had gone down that path would you have said yes?' His lips twisted with mocking superiority. 'If I had romanced you, Aspen, I could have had you naked and beneath me in a matter of hours and saved myself a hell of a lot of money.'

Aspen threw him a withering look, ignoring the sudden mental picture of them both naked and tangled together. 'You can save yourself a hell of a lot of money *and* skin right now and get off my property,' she said tightly.

His nostrils flared as he breathed deeply and she suddenly realised how close he was, how far she had to tilt her head back to look up at him. 'And for your information,' she began, wanting to stamp all over his supersized ego, 'I would *never* have said yes to you.'

'Really?'

He stepped even closer and Aspen felt the harsh bite of wood at her back. Caged, she could only stare as Cruz lifted one of her spiral curls again; this time carrying it to his nose. Her hands rose to shove him back but he didn't budge, and almost immediately her senses tuned in to the warm packed muscle beneath the thin cotton of his shirt, to the fast beat of his heart that seemed to mirror her own racing pulse.

A flash of memory took her back eight years to the feel of his mouth on hers. The feel of his tongue rubbing hers. The feel of his hands spanning her waist. Heat pooled inside her and made her breasts heavy, her legs unsteady. She remembered that after they'd been caught she had been so shocked by her physical reaction to him and so scared of her grandfather's wrath she'd fallen utterly silent—ashamed of herself for considering one man's marriage proposal while losing herself in the arms of another. Cruz hadn't raised one word of denial the whole time and she still wondered why.

Not that she had time to consider that now… He leant forward as if her staying hands were nothing more than crepe paper. His breath brushed her ear.

'Let me tell you what I remember, *gatita*. I remember the way your curvy backside filled out those tight jodhpurs. I remember the purple bikini top you used to wear riding your horse along the beach. And I remember the way you used to watch me. A bit like the way you were watching me stroke the mare before.' His hand tightened in her hair. 'You were thinking about how it would feel if I put my hands on you again, weren't you? How it would feel if I kissed you?'

Aspen made a half coughing noise in instant denial and tried to catch her breath. There was no way he could have known she'd been thinking exactly that.

'Have you turned into a dreamer, Cruz?' she mocked with false bravado, frightened beyond belief at how vulnerable she suddenly felt. 'Because really a dream would be the only place I would ever want something like that from you.'

Dreamer?

Cruz felt his jaw knot at her insolent tone. How dared she accuse him of being a dreamer when *she* was clearly the dreamer here if she thought she could buy and hold onto the rundown estate Ocean Haven had become?

Memories of the past swirled around him and bit deep. Memories of how she had felt in his arms. How she had tasted. Memories of how she had stood there, all dazed innocence, and listened to her grandfather rail at him. He'd been accused of ruining her that night but it was her—her and that slimy fiancé of hers, Chad Anderson—who had tried to ruin him. She and her lover who had set him up for a fall to clear the way for Chad to take over as captain of Charles Carmichael's dream team.

There'd been no other explanation for it, and he'd always wondered how far she would have taken things if her grandfather had turned up five minutes later. Because that was all it would have taken for him to twist her nightie up past her hips and thrust deep into her velveteen warmth.

His eyes took her in now. Her defiant expression and flushed face. Her rapidly beating pulse and her moist lips where her pink tongue had just lashed them. Her hands were burning a hole in his shirt and he was already as hard as stone—and, by God, he'd had enough of her holier-than-thou attitude.

'You would have loved it.' Cruz twisted her hair into a knot at the back of her head and pulled her roughly up against him. '*Will* love it,' he promised thickly, wrapping his other arm around her waist and staunching her shocked cry with his mouth.

Her lips immediately clamped together and she pushed against him, but that only brought her body more fully up against his as her hands slipped over his shoulders. She stilled, as if the added contact affected her as much as it affected him, and with a deep groan he ran his tongue across the seam of her lips. He felt a shiver run through her and then she shoved harder to dislodge him. He told himself he wasn't doing his plan any favours by forcing himself on her, but the plan paled into insignificance when compared to the feel of her warm and wriggling in his arms. He wanted her to surrender to him. To admit that the chemistry that had exploded through him like a haze of bloodlust as soon as he had seen her again wasn't just one-sided.

But some inner instinct warned him that this wasn't the way to get her to acquiesce, and years of experience in gentling horses rushed through him. He marshalled some of that strength and patience now and gentled her. Sucking at her lips, nipping, soothing her with his tongue. She made a tiny whimper in the back of her throat and he felt a sense of primal victory as she tentatively opened her mouth under his, aligning her body so that her soft curves were no longer resisting his hardness but melting against him until he could feel every sweet, feminine inch of her.

With a low growl of approval he gentled his hold on her and angled her head so that he could take her mouth more fully. When her lips opened wider and her arms urged him closer he couldn't stop himself from plundering her, couldn't resist drawing her tongue out so that she could taste him in return.

An unexpected sense of completeness settled over him—a sense of finding something he'd been searching for his whole life—and he didn't want the kiss to end. He didn't want this maddening arousal to end.

If he'd had any idea that it would be like this again he wasn't sure that he would have started it. But now that he had he didn't want to stop. *Ever.* She tasted so sweet. So silky. So *good.*

He made a sound low in his throat when she circled her pelvis against his in an age-old request and he couldn't think after that. Could only grab her hips and smooth his hands over her firm backside to mould her against him.

'Yes,' he whispered roughly against her mouth. 'Kiss me, *chiquita*. Give me everything.'

And she did. Without reservation. Her mouth devouring his as if she too had dreamed of this over and over and over. As if she too couldn't live without—

'Ow!'

Her sharp cry of pain echoed his deeper one as something pushed the back of his head and bumped his forehead into hers. He pulled back and glared over his shoulder to where the horse he had just agreed to purchase snorted in disgust.

Aspen blinked dazedly, rubbing at her head. Then the stunned look on her face cleared and he knew their impromptu little make out session had well and truly finished.

'You bastard.'

She raised her arm and slapped his face. The sound echoed in the cavernous stall and he worked his jaw as heat bloomed where her palm had connected.

About to tell her that she had a good arm, he was shocked to see that she had turned white and looked as if she might pass out.

'Aspen?'

She looked at him as if *he* had hit *her*. 'Now look what you made me do!' she cried.

Well, wasn't that typical of her—to blame him?

'I didn't *make* you do anything. You hit me. And if I'm not mistaken all because you enjoyed my kisses just a little too much.'

'Oh!'

She pushed against him with all her might and he was only too glad to step away from her.

'I've already turned down one slimy rat today and now I'm turning down another.' Her glare alone could have buried him. 'Now, get off my property before I have every man available throw you off.'

'I'm flattered you think it would take that many.'

'Oh, I bet you are.' Every inch of her trembled with feminine outrage. 'But I'm not prepared to take chances with a bully like you.'

'I didn't bully you, *chiquita*. You were asking for it.'

'Don't call me that.'

Cruz rubbed his jaw and scowled. 'What?'

'You know what.'

His brain must still have been on a go-slow because he couldn't recall what he'd called her. The thought irked him enough that he said, 'Maybe you should think about the way you act and dress if you don't want men thinking you're free and easy in bed.'

'Oh, my God. Are you serious?'

'Silky dresses that outline every curve, killer heels and just-out-of-bed hair all tell a man what's what.'

Fascinated, he watched her pull herself up to her full five feet and four inches—six in the heels.

'Any man who judges me on the way I look isn't worth a dime. You and Billy—'

Cruz raised his hand, cutting short her dramatic tirade. 'I am not like him,' he snarled.

'Keep telling yourself that, Cruz.' She tossed her head at him. 'It might help you sleep better at night.'

'I sleep just fine,' he grated. 'But if you should decide to change your high and mighty little mind about my offer I'll be staying at the Boston International until tomorrow morning.'

'Don't hold your breath.' She reefed open the stall door and stomped past him. 'I'd have to be crazy to accept an offer like that.'

Cruz ran a shaky hand through his hair and listened to the staccato sound of her high heels hammering her ire against the stone floor.

Her words, 'don't hold your breath' rang out in his head. Hadn't he told his brother the same thing a few hours ago? *Hell.* If he had, he couldn't remember why.

CHAPTER FOUR

'Dammit.' Aspen cursed as her hair caught around the button she had just wrenched open on the front of her dress. 'Stupid, idiotic hair.'

She yanked at it and winced when she heard the telltale crackle that indicated that she'd left a chunk behind. Then the pain set in and she rubbed her scalp.

God, she was angry. Furious. She pulled at the rest of her buttons and stopped when she caught sight of herself in the free-standing mirror that stood in the corner of her bedroom. Slowly she walked towards it.

An ordinary female figure stared back. An ordinary female figure with a flushed face and a wild mane of horrible hair. And tender lips. She put her fingers to them. They *looked* the same as they always did, but they *felt* softer. Swollen. And there was a slight graze on her chin where Cruz's stubble had scraped her skin.

Her pelvis clenched at the remembered pleasure of his mouth on hers. He hadn't even kissed her like that eight years ago. Then he'd been softer, almost tender. Today he'd kissed her as if he hadn't been able to help himself. As if he'd wanted to devour her. And never before had she kissed someone like that in return. Thank God Gypsy Blue had tried to knock some sense into them.

She had no idea why she'd acted like that with a man who had insulted her so badly. Maybe it was the fact that seeing him again had knocked her sideways. Somehow he had dazzled her the way he'd used to dazzle the women at polo matches. He was so attractive the crowds had always doubled when he had played, because all the wives and girlfriends had insisted that they simply *loved* polo and had to spend the *whole* day watching it. Really, they'd just mooned over him when he'd been on the field and drunk champagne and chatted the rest of the time. He'd dazzled her friends too.

Unconsciously she licked her tender lips and felt his imprint on them. Really she felt his imprint everywhere—and especially in the space between her thighs.

Heaven help her! She would have had sex with him. Had inadvertently *wanted* to have sex with him. The realisation of that alone was enough to shock her. She hated sex!

So why was she currently reliving Cruz's wicked kisses over and over like a hopeless teenager? He hadn't kissed her out of any real passion—he'd kissed her to make a point and to put her in her place and by God she had let him! Putting up a token resistance like the Victorian virgin he had accused her of acting like and then melting all over him like hot syrup.

She scratched the hair at her temples and made her curls frizz. Grabbing the offending matter, she quickly braided it, pulled on her jeans and shirt and stomped down to the stables.

Donny raised a startled eyebrow as she muttered a few terse words in his direction and started work at the other end. The rhythmical physical labour of putting away tack and shifting hay, of bantering with the horses and going through the motions of bedding them down for the night, was doing nothing to eradicate the feeling of all that hard male muscle pressed up against her.

'Make sure you don't burn your bridges unnecessarily, Aspen. Pride can be a nasty thing when it's used rashly.'

Pride? What pride. She had none. Well, she'd had enough to say no to both him and Billy Smyth.

'Oh, Billy Smyth! There's no way I would have slept with him even if he wasn't married,' she told Delta as she brushed her down vigorously.

But you would have with Cruz Rodriguez. Even without the money.

'I would not,' she promised Delta, knowing that if she had sex again with any man it would be too soon.

She stopped and leant her forehead against the mare. She breathed in her comforting scent and stared out over the stall door, looking up when something—a rat, maybe—disturbed a sleeping pigeon.

Her eye was immediately drawn to a rusty horseshoe lodged firmly between two supporting beams. Her mother had told her the story about how it had got there when she was little and it was the first thing Aspen had looked for when she had come to Ocean Haven, missing her mother desperately. Since then, whenever she was in a tricky situation she came out here and sought her mother's advice.

'And, boy, do I need it right now,' she muttered.

Delta nudged her side, as if to tell her to get on with it.

'Yes, I know.' She patted her neck. 'I'm thinking.'

Thinking about how much this place meant to her. Thinking about the dreams she had that would never materialise if she lost it. And she would lose it. To some faceless consortium in five days. Her stomach felt as if it had a rock in it.

Cruz's offer crept back into her mind for the thousandth time. He was right; it was pride making her say no.

So what if she said yes?

No, she couldn't. Cruz was big and overpowering and arrogant. Exactly the type of man she'd vowed to keep well away from.

But you're not marrying him.

No, but she would have to sleep with him. Which was just as unpalatable.

Sighing, she contemplated the peeling paint on the stall door. Her mother's face swam into her mind. Her tired smile. The day she had died she had been so exhausted after working two jobs and caring for Aspen, who had been sick at the time, that she'd simply forgotten that cars drove on the left-hand side of the road in England and she'd stepped out onto a busy road. It had been horrific. Devastating.

Aspen felt a pang of remorse and a deep longing. She had to keep Ocean Haven if only to preserve her mother's memory.

Feeling weighted down by memories, she continued brushing Delta. She had eked out a life here. She felt whole here. Protected. And, dammit, if she could keep it she would. She hadn't worked this hard to lose everything now.

Rash pride.

Rash pride had stopped her grandfather and her mother from reaching out to each other and maybe changing their lives for the better. Rash pride had made her grandfather refuse to listen to her own concerns about Chad after she had mentioned her doubts to him right before the wedding.

Rash pride wasn't going to get in the way of her life decisions any more. If Cruz Rodriguez wanted her body he could damned well have it. She didn't care. She hadn't cared about that side of things for years. And, anyway, once he found out what a dud she was in bed he'd change his mind pretty quickly.

Familiar fingers of distaste crawled up her spine as she recalled her wedding night before she could prevent herself doing it. She swallowed. What surprised her most was that being in Cruz's arms had been nothing like being in Chad's. But then Chad had often been drunk during their brief marriage and the alcohol had changed him. After that first night Aspen had frozen so much on the rare occasions he had approached her that he'd sought solace elsewhere. And made sure she knew about it. Always being deeply apologetic the following day when the alcoholic haze had retreated.

She'd stayed with him for six months and tried to be a better wife, but then he'd unfairly accused her of sleeping with his patron. It had been the final straw and she'd fled to Ocean Haven and never looked back.

She shivered.

'If you should happen to change your high and mighty little mind I'll be staying at the Boston International until tomorrow morning.'

Had she changed her mind?

There was no doubt that Cruz hated her after what had happened eight years ago, but he must also want her to make such an extreme offer. Could she put her concerns aside and sleep with him? She already knew she responded differently with him, felt differently with him, but what if she froze at the last minute as she had with Chad? What if he laughed at her when he learned about her embarrassing problem?

Rash pride, Aspen...

She groaned. To find out was to experiment, and to experiment meant opening herself up to knowing once and for all that *she* had been the problem in the bedroom and not Chad—as she sometimes liked to pretend when she was feeling particularly low.

'Coward,' she said softly.

Delta whickered.

'Oh, not you, beauty.' Aspen fished inside her pocket for a sugar cube. 'You're brave and courageous and would probably not bat an eyelid if I told you that Ranger's Apprentice had paid money to mount you if it meant saving The Farm.'

Aspen unwound Delta's tail from the tight bundle it had been wrapped in for the polo and wondered what would become of her beloved horses if she had to leave. Wondered if they'd be well cared for.

She felt she should warn the unsuspecting mare. 'If I keep The Farm I probably will be putting you in with him next season. I hope you don't mind. He's quite handsome.'

Not that looks had anything to do with the price of eggs.

She sighed as Donny stopped by Delta's stall and said that his lot were all set for the night and he would help out with some of the others if Aspen needed it.

At the rate she was going Aspen would need an army to get the horses done before the week was out.

She smiled at him. He had worked on the farm for six years now and she'd be lost without him. 'You're a gem, but I'm good. You go home to Glenda and the kids.'

'You're sure?' He shifted his gum around in his mouth. 'You seem a little wound up.'

Oh, she was. Ten million dollars wound up.

'Donny, what would you do if everything you loved was being threatened?' she asked suddenly.

He stuck a finger through his belt buckle and considered his shoes. 'You mean like Glenda and Sasha and Lela? Like my home?'

'Yeah,' Aspen said softly. 'Like your home.'

Donny nodded. 'I'd fight if I could.'

Aspen smiled. 'That's what I thought.'

Donny turned to go and then looked back over his shoulder. 'You sure you're all right, boss?'

'Fine. See you Monday.'

Cruz was going crazy. When a man let his ego get in the way of common sense that was the only conclusion to make. And the only one that made sense.

What other explanation could there possibly be when

he had just offered a woman he didn't even like ten million dollars to sleep with him?

And what would he have done if she'd said yes? Because he'd had no intention of going through with it. The very idea was ludicrous. He'd never paid for sex in his life.

So he wanted her? Big deal. It was because she was even more alluring than he remembered. And more stuck-up. Her hair was longer too, her cheekbones more defined, her breasts fuller, her mouth— He laughed. What was he doing? A full inventory? Why? There were plenty of women in his sea. Plenty more beautiful than this one when it came down to it.

And, yes, he liked to pit himself against an opponent for the sheer thrill of it, but making that offer to Aspen Carmichael had felt a bit like riding a nag into the middle of a forty-goal polo game without a bridle or a saddle and telling his opponents to have at him.

He certainly hadn't come anywhere close to finding a way to ensure that she wouldn't be able to raise the money to buy Ocean Haven herself—which had been his original goal.

Cruz poked at the half-eaten steak sandwich on his plate and stuffed an overcooked chip into his mouth. All he'd done instead was lump himself in with the likes of Billy Smyth and he was nothing like his lot.

No, you're worse, his conscience happily informed him. *You'd like to screw her* and *steal her family home out from under her as well.*

Yeah, whatever.

Unused to having a back and forth commentary inside his head about a woman—or about his decisions—he shoved himself to his feet and headed outside to see if the answer to his problem was written in the stars.

Of course it wasn't, but he stood there and let the warm evening air wash over him until memories of the past sailed in on the scent of jasmine and lilac. The sickening ball that had settled in his gut as he'd driven through the stone archway to Ocean Haven returned full force.

Focusing on something else, he listened to the distant murmurs of the light-hearted partying he could hear coming up off the darkened beach. Probably teenagers enjoying yet another stunning summer evening. Light flickered and wisps of smoke trailed in the moonlight. He imagined that many of them would be pairing off before long and snuggling down beside a campfire.

Unbidden, his mind conjured up an image of Aspen flirting with Billy Smyth earlier that day. He'd watched them for a couple of minutes before approaching her, not really wanting anyone to recognise him and start fawning all over him.

Aspen had used all her feminine wiles so the unhappily married Billy would notice her, but it hadn't been until she had let him run his finger down the side of her face and held her cheek afterwards, as if preserving his touch, that real bitterness and anger had rolled through Cruz like an incoming thunderstorm. Would she have let Smyth kiss her and shove her up against the wall of the stable as she had done with him earlier? Had she *planned* to later on?

'Damn her anyway.' He slammed the palm of his hand against the bronze railing and told himself to forget about her. Forget about the way she had caught fire in his arms once again. Forget about the way he had done the same in hers. Unfortunately his body was more than happy to relive it, and he was once again uncomfortably hard as he headed inside and downed the rest of his tequila.

As far as Cruz was concerned the Aspen Carmichaels of the world deserved everything they got. So why was he hanging around his hotel room feeling like the worst kind of male alive?

No reason.

No reason at all.

The hotel phone rang and he crossed to the hall table and picked it up, almost disappointed to find that the number on the display was a local one. Because he knew who it was even before he answered it. And now was the time to tell her that he had no intention of giving her the money in exchange for her delectable body. No intention at all.

But he didn't say that. Instead he threw his conscience to the wind and said, 'I'll pick you up at seven in the morning.'

There was enough of a silence on the other end of the line for him to wonder if he hadn't been mistaken, but then Aspen's husky tones sounded in his ear.

'Why?'

'Because I'm flying back to Mexico first thing in the morning.'

She cleared her throat. 'I can wait until you're next in Boston.'

She might be able to. He couldn't.

'You need that money by Monday, don't you?'

Again there was a pause long enough to fill the Grand Canyon. He waited for her to tell him to go to hell.

'Yes,' she said as if she was grinding nails.

'I'll see you tomorrow, then.'

He hung up before she could say anything else and stood staring at the telephone. He didn't know what shocked him more: the fact that he hadn't rescinded his ludicrous offer or the fact that he had made it in the first place. What didn't shock him was the fact that she had accepted.

He waited for a sense of satisfaction to kick in because he had finally come up with a way to stop her going after anyone else for the money. Instead he felt a sense of impending doom. Like a man who had bitten off more than he could chew. Because he had no intention of lending her the money and he didn't like what that said about him.

Maybe that he needed more tequila.

'Just have a shower, *imbecil,* and get some sleep,' he told himself.

Come Saturday The Rodriquez Polo Club would run the biggest polo tournament in Mexico for the second year and he had a Chinese delegation coming over to view the proceedings. They had some notion that he could form a partnership with them to introduce polo into China via a specialised hotel in Beijing. So he had to be on site for the next three days and be at his charming best.

'Better get rid of the *chica*, then,' he told his reflection grimly as he stripped off and stepped into the shower. Because watching Aspen flick her hair and flirt with everything in pants was not, he already knew, conducive to putting him in a good mood.

Ah, hell, maybe he should just forget the whole thing. Forget buying Ocean Haven. Yes, it was an exceptional piece of land, with those rolling hills and the bluff that looked out over the North Atlantic Ocean. But there were plenty of beautiful spots in the world. What did he really want it for anyway?

He squirted shampoo over his head and rubbed vigorously.

The fact was eight years ago Aspen Carmichael had set him up so that her over-indulged fiancé could take his place on the dream team without batting a pretty eyelash. She'd walked up to him and shyly put her arms around his neck and, like a fool who had fantasised about her for too long, he'd lost control. He would have done anything for her back then because, if he was honest, he'd liked her a little bit himself. Liked her a lot, in fact, and he hated knowing that she'd so easily fooled him.

But not this time. This time he would be the one holding all the cards. He relaxed for the first time that night. And why not? Why not take what she had offered him eight years ago? She was older now, and obviously still prepared to use her delectable body to get what she wanted. *So, okay—game on, Ms Carmichael. Game on.*

And if a small voice in his head said that he was wrong about her—well, he couldn't see how.

So what that she had loved the horses and been kind to everyone she came into contact with? So what if her apology earlier had seemed genuine? She knew how to play the game, that was all *that* said about her, but in the end she'd used him for her own ends just like everyone else in his life had done.

So, no, he didn't owe Aspen-damned-Carmichael any-damned-thing. And if this was fate's way of evening the score between them then, hell, who was he to argue?

CHAPTER FIVE

ASPEN WAS PACKED and ready by six the following morning. She'd told Mrs Randall, their long-time housekeeper, that she was going to Mexico to look over Cruz's horses for future growth opportunities. It was the best explanation she could come up with at short notice, especially when Mrs Randall had looked so pleased at the mention of Cruz's name.

'He missed his family terribly, that boy. Of course he was too proud to show it, but I suppose that was why he left so suddenly when he was a young man. He wanted to get back to them.'

Aspen would have liked to believe that homesickness had contributed to Cruz leaving The Farm eight years ago, but she suspected it was more because she had put him in an untenable situation.

Guilt ate at her, and all the confusing emotions she'd experienced at that time came rushing back. Her desperate need for approval from her grandfather, her fear of the future, her confusing feelings for Chad and the amazing pull she'd always felt towards Cruz.

Fortunately Mrs Randall was doing her Thursday morning market shopping when Cruz drove up in a mean black sports car, because Aspen was sure her confused state would have been on display for the wily older woman to see and that would have only added to her anxiety. Especially when she had decided that the best way to approach the situation was to be optimistic and positive. Treat it as the business transaction it was.

Shielded by the velvet drapes in the living room, she watched as Cruz climbed out of the car and literally prowled towards the front steps of the house, breathtakingly handsome in worn jeans that clung to his muscular thighs and a fitted latte-coloured T-shirt that set off his olive skin tone and black hair to perfection.

Not wanting him to think she was nervous at the prospect of seeing him, Aspen waited a few minutes after he'd pressed the bell before opening the door; glad that just last week she had given the front door a fresh lick of white paint and cleaned down the stone façade of the portico with an industrial hose.

'Good morning.' She hoped he hadn't heard her voice quaver and told herself that if she was really going to go through with this she needed to do better than she was now. 'Did you want coffee or tea?'

His gaze swept over her face and lingered on her chin, and when he unconsciously rubbed his jaw she knew he had noticed the mark—*his* mark—that she had made a futile effort to cover with concealer. Involuntarily her own eyes dropped to his mouth and heat coursed through her; she was mortified and embarrassed when his lips tightened with dismissal and he turned abruptly to scan the rest of the hallway.

'No. My plane's on standby. Let's go.'

Great. She wasn't even going to have the benefit of other commuters to ease the journey.

Turning to pick up her keys from the hallway table, she spotted the document she had spent half the night drafting. She couldn't believe she'd forgotten it. But then rational thinking and Cruz Rodriguez didn't seem to go together for her very well.

'I'd like you to sign this first.'

He looked at it dubiously. 'What is it?'

It was a document stipulating a condition she hoped he'd agree to and also preventing him from reneging on their deal if he found himself dissatisfied with the outcome of their temporary liaison. Which he undoubtedly would. But since this was a business arrangement Aspen wanted to make sure that when their physical relationship failed he was still bound to invest in Ocean Haven.

'Read it. I think it's clear enough.'

He took it from her and the paper snapped in the quiet room. The antique grandfather clock gauged time like a marksman.

It wasn't long before he glanced back at her, and Aspen swallowed as he laughed out loud.

Her mouth tightened as she waited for him to collect himself. She'd had an idea that he might have some objections to her demands but she hadn't expected that he find them comical.

'Once?' His eyes were full of amusement. 'Are you're kidding me?'

She wasn't. *Once*, she was sure, was going to be more than enough for both of them.

'No.'

When he looked as if he might start laughing again Aspen felt her nerves give way to temper.

'I don't see what's so funny?'

'That's because you're not paying the money.'

He circled behind her as if she was some slave girl on an auction block and he was checking her over.

She swung around to face him. 'If you read the whole document it says that I'm planning to pay you back the money anyway, so technically it's free.'

'With what?'

He unnerved her by circling her again, but this time she stood stock-still. 'I don't know what you mean.'

'What are you intending to pay me back with?' he murmured from behind her.

'The profits from The Farm.'

He scoffed, facing her. 'This place will be lucky to break even in a booming market.'

His eyes held hers and the chemistry that was as strong as carbon links every time they got within two feet of each other flared hotly. Aspen took a careful breath in. He was pure Alpha male right now, and his self-satisfied smile let her know that *he* knew the effect he was having on her.

Not that it would help either one of them in the long run. But she had to concentrate. If she didn't there was a chance she'd end up with nothing. Less than nothing. Because she'd lose the only tie she had left to her mother.

'That's your opinion. It's not mine.'

He studied her and she didn't know how she managed not to squirm under that penetrating gaze.

'It would want to be a damned good once, *gatita*.'

Aspen raised her chin. It was going to be horrible.

'It's a good deal.' She repeated what she'd said to Billy Smyth and so many others before him. 'Take it or leave it.'

He regarded her steadily, his eyes hooded. 'I tell you what. You make it one night and I'll agree.'

One night?

'As in the *whole* night?'

His slow smile sent a burst of electrical activity straight to her core. 'What a good idea, *gatita*. Yes, the whole night.'

Bastard.

'What *is* that you're calling me?' she fumed.

His smile was full of sex. '*Kitten*. You remind me of a spitting kitten who needs to be stroked.'

'Fine.' Aspen picked up the pen but didn't see a thing in front of her.

'Wait. Before you make your changes I want to know what this is.' Cruz stabbed his finger at her second point—the one that said he had to pay no matter what happened or didn't happen between them. 'Is this your way of telling me you're going to welsh on me?'

She frowned. 'Welsh on you?'

'Renege. Back out. Break your word.'

'I know what it means,' she snapped, wondering if he wasn't having a go at her character. 'And rest assured I am fully prepared to uphold my end of the bargain. I just want to make sure you do as well.'

Her throat bobbed as he continued to watch her and Cruz wondered if she had guessed that he was stringing her along.

Once!

He nearly laughed again. But he had to hand it to her. The document she had crafted was legally sound and would probably hold up well enough in a court of law.

Something about the way she stood before him, all innocently defiant, like a lamb to the slaughter, snagged on his conscience like an annoying burr in a sock, which you'd thought you'd removed only to have it poke at you again.

He couldn't do it. He couldn't let her go into this blind. 'There's something you should know.'

Her eyes turned wary. 'Like what?'

'I own Trimex Holdings.'

Aspen frowned. 'If that's supposed to mean something to me it doesn't.'

'Trimex Holdings is currently the highest bidder for Ocean Haven.'

He watched a myriad of emotions flit across her expressive face as the information set in. Shock. Disbelief. Anger. Uncertainty.

'So…' She frowned harder. 'This isn't real?'

How much he wanted her? Unfortunately, yes.

He tried not to let his gaze drop once again to the spot on her chin. He'd obviously grazed her with his stubble the day before and, although he'd hate to think that he'd hurt her, there was a part of him that was pretty pleased to see her wearing his mark. The moronic part.

Oh, yeah, it was real enough. But he knew that wasn't what she was referring to.

'My offer?'

'Yes.'

'It's real.'

'That doesn't make sense. Why would you lend me money to buy a property you are trying to buy for yourself?'

'Because I believe I'll win.' And he had just decided to instruct Lauren to keep upping his offer until it was so ludicrously tempting Joe Carmichael would see stars.

Aspen shook her head. 'You won't. Joe is very loyal to me.'

All families were loyal until money was involved. 'Care to back yourself?'

She looked at him as one might a maggot on a pork chop. 'I never realised how absolutely ruthless you are.'

'I'm absolutely successful. For a reason.'

She shook her head. 'You're not going to be this time. But can I trust you?'

The fact that she questioned his integrity annoyed him. 'I didn't have to tell you this, did I?'

'Fine,' she snapped, pacing away from him to the other side of the neat sitting room. She glared at him. Shook her head. Then paced back. Picked up the pen. 'It's not like I have a better option right now.'

Her fingers shook ever so slightly as she put pen to paper and something squeezed inside his chest.

'I'll do it.'

Impatient for this to be finalised, he grabbed the pen and replaced 'once' with 'one night'. Then he scrawled the date and his signature on the bottom of the page.

His gaze drifted down over her neat summer tunic which showed the delicate hollows either side of her collarbones and hinted at her firm breasts before it skimmed the tops of her feminine thighs. She'd been soft and firm pressed up against him yesterday. Svelte, he decided, glancing at her fitted jeans and ankle boots.

His body reacted predictably and he told himself it was past time to stop looking at her.

The flight from East Hampton to Acapulco took five hours. It might as well have been five days. Cruz had barely uttered a word to her since leaving The Farm—not much more than 'This way', 'Mind your step' and 'Buckle up; we're about to take off'. And Aspen was glad. She didn't think she'd be able to hold a decent conversation with the man right now. He wasn't a rat, she decided. He was a shark. A great white that hunted and killed without compunction.

And she was playing the game of her life against him.

Thank heavens she had her uncle on her side. But could she trust Cruz to give her the money? He'd looked startled and not a little angry when she had questioned his integrity. Yes, she was pretty sure she could trust him. His pride alone would mean that he upheld his end of the deal.

The deal. She had just made a bargain to sleep with the devil. She shuddered, glancing across the aisle to where Cruz was seated in a matching plush leather chair and buried in paperwork. It was beyond her comprehension that she should still want him. Which was scary in itself when she considered that she didn't even like sex. And, yes, she'd enjoyed kissing him, but that wasn't sex. She knew if they'd been anywhere near a bed she would have clammed up.

Urgh… She hated the thought of embarrassing herself in front of him. He was so confident. So *arrogant*. She hated that he just had to look at her and she had to concentrate extra hard to think logically. His touching her made her want to do stupid things. Things she couldn't trust.

And she particularly hated the thought of being vulnerable to him. Especially now. Now when he had made it clear that he'd win anyway. That she was doing this for nothing. It just made her more determined that he wouldn't.

Aspen pulled out her textbook. Questioning whether she had done the right thing in coming with him wouldn't change anything now. She'd signed the document she herself had drafted and she'd assured him that she wouldn't 'welsh' on him.

It would mean that her beloved home was hers. It would mean she would have the chance to put all the naysayers who didn't believe that a girl on her own could run a property the size of Ocean Haven in their places. And it would mean that for the first time in her life she would be free and clear of a dominating man controlling her future. That alone would be worth a little embarrassment with the Latin bad boy she had once fantasised about.

It was a thought that wasn't easy to hold onto when the plane landed on a private airstrip and a blast of hot, humid air swept across her face.

Cruz's long, loose-limbed strides ate up the tarmac as if the humid air hadn't just hit him like a furnace. He stopped by a waiting four-by-four and Aspen kept her eyes anywhere but on him as she climbed inside, doing her best to ease the kinks out of shoulders aching with tension.

Still, she noticed when he put on a pair of aviator sunglasses and clasped another man's hands in a display of macho camaraderie before taking the keys from him.

He was just so self-assured, she thought enviously, and she hated him. Hated him and everything he represented. Yesterday she'd been willing to greet him as a friend, had felt sorry for the part she had played in his leaving The Farm. Now she wished her grandfather had horsewhipped him. It was the least he deserved.

But did he?

Just because he wanted to buy her farm it didn't make him a bad guy, did it? No, not necessarily bad—but ruthless. And arrogant. And so handsome it hurt to look at him.

'You know I hate you, don't you?' she said without thinking.

Not bothering to look at her, he paused infinitesimally, his hands on the key in the ignition.

'Probably,' he said, with so little concern it made her teeth grind together.

He turned the key and the car purred to life. Then his eyes drifted lazily over her from head to toe and she felt her heart-rate kick up. He was studying her again. Looking at her as if he was imagining what she looked like without her clothes on.

'But it won't make a difference.'

His lack of empathy, or any real emotion, drove her wild. 'To what?'

'To this.'

Quick as a flash he reached for her, grabbed the back of her neck before she'd realised his intention and hauled her mouth across to his. Aspen stiffened, determined to resist the force of his hungry assault. And she did. For a moment. A brief moment before her senses took over and shut down her brain. A brief moment before his mouth softened. A brief moment before he pulled back and looked at her with lazy amusement. As if he was already the victor.

'He won't sell to you,' she blazed at him.

His smile kicked up one corner of his mouth. 'He'll sell to me.'

Aspen cut her gaze from his. She hated his insolent confidence because she wished she had just a smidgeon of it herself. 'How long till we get there?' she griped.

He laughed softly. 'So eager, *gatita*?'

'Yes,' she fumed. 'Eager to get out of your horrible company. In fact I don't know why we didn't just do this on the plane. Or at The Farm, come to think of it.'

His head tilted as he regarded her. 'Maybe I want to woo you.'

Aspen blew out a breath. 'I wonder what your mother would have to say about your behaviour?'

'Damn.' Cruz forked a hand through his hair, his lazy amusement at her expense turning to disgust.

He cursed again and gunned the engine.

'Problem?' she asked, hoping beyond hope that there was one.

'You could say that.' His words came out as a snarl.

She waited for him to elaborate and sighed when he didn't. This situation was impossible. There was no way she would be able to relax with this man enough to have sex with him. Which was fine, she thought. It would serve him right, all things considered.

Switching her mind off, she turned her attention outside the window. From the air Mexico was an amazing contrast of stark brown mountains and stretches of dried-up desert against the brilliant blue of the Pacific Ocean. On the ground the theme continued, with pockets of abject beauty mixed with states of disrepair. A bit like her own mind, she mused in a moment of black humour.

But gradually, as Cruz drove them through small towns and along broken cobblestoned streets alive with pedestrians and tourists fortified against the amazing heat with wide-brimmed hats, Aspen felt herself start to relax.

She snuck a glance at Cruz's beautiful profile. His expression was so serious he looked as if he belonged on a penny. The silence stretched out like the bitumen in front of them and finally Aspen couldn't take it any longer. 'So you went back to Mexico after you left The Farm?'

He cut her a brief glance. 'You want the low-down on my life story, *gatita*?'

No, she wanted to know if it would take a silver bullet to end his life, or whether an ordinary one would do the trick.

One night, Aspen.

'I was making polite conversation.'

'Choose another topic.'

Okay.

'Why do you want my farm?'

'It's a great location for a hotel. Why else?'

Aspen glared at him. 'You're going to tear it down, aren't you?' Tear down the only home she'd ever loved. Tear down the stables.

'Perhaps.'

'You can't do that.'

'Actually, I can.'

'Why? Revenge?'

She saw a muscle tick in his jaw. 'Not revenge. Money.'

Aspen blew out a breath, more determined than ever that he shouldn't get his hands on her property. 'How much further is it to the hotel?' she asked completely exasperated.

Cruz smiled. 'You sound like you're not expecting to enjoy yourself, *gatita*.'

She didn't answer, and she felt his curious gaze on her as she stared sightlessly out of the window.

'It will be a while,' he said abruptly. 'We have a small detour to make.'

Aspen glanced back at his austere expression. 'What sort of detour?'

'I have to stop at my mother's house.'

'Your mother's house?' She frowned. 'Why would you take me to meet your mother?'

'Believe me, I'm not happy about it either,' he said. 'Unfortunately my brother has arranged her surprise birthday party for today and I promised I'd show up.'

'Your mother's…' She cleared her throat as if she had something stuck in it. 'You could have warned me.'

'I just did.'

She blew out a frustrated breath.

'Don't make a big deal out of it,' he cautioned. 'I'm not.'

'Well, that's obvious. But how can I not? What will she think of me?'

'That you're my latest mistress. What else?'

Cruz saw a flash of hurt cross her face and hated how she made him feel subtly guilty about the situation between them. He had nothing to feel guilty about. She had asked him for money, he had laid down his terms, and she'd accepted. And now that she knew he was in direct competition with her his conscience was clear. Or should have been. Still, it picked at him that he might be making a decision he would later regret. His body said the opposite and he ran his eyes over her feminine, but demure outfit. All that wild hair caught back in a low ponytail just begging to be set free.

'I don't have anything for her,' she said in a small voice.

Cruz forced himself to concentrate on a particularly dilapidated section of road before he had an accident. 'I've got it covered.'

She fell blessedly silent after that as he navigated through the centre of town and he was just exhaling when she spoke again.

'What did you get her?'

'Excuse me?'

'Your present. I would know what it was if I was really your mistress.'

'You *are* my mistress,' he reminded her. 'For one night anyway.'

If possible even more colour drained from her face, and it irritated him to think that she saw sleeping with him as such a chore. By the time he was finished with her she would be screaming with pleasure and begging for more than one night.

'Money,' he said, pulling his thoughts out of his pants.

'Sorry?'

'I'm giving her money.'

'Oh.'

Her nose twitched as if she'd just smelt something foul.

'What's wrong with that?' he snapped.

'Nothing.'

Her tone implied *everything*.

'Money makes the world go round, *gatita*,' he grated.

'Actually, I think the saying is that love makes the world go round.'

'Love couldn't make a tennis ball go round,' he said, knowing from her tight expression that she didn't approve or agree. Well, he didn't give a damn. *She* hadn't been given up as a child. 'Look, my mother sold me to your grandfather when I was thirteen. I think I know what she likes.'

Aspen looked aghast. 'I had heard that rumour but I never actually believed it.'

'Believe it,' he said, hating the note of bitterness that tinged his words.

'I'm sure she didn't *want* to send you away.'

Cruz didn't say anything. She sighed and eventually said, 'I know how you feel.'

'How could you possibly know how I feel?' he mocked.

'You grew up on a hundred-acre property and went to a private school.'

'I wasn't born into that, Cruz. My father left my mother when I was three and she struggled for years to keep our heads above water while she was alive. What I was getting at was that my grandfather paid my father to stay away.'

Cruz frowned. He'd assumed her mother had lived off some sort of trust fund and her father had died. 'Your father was a ski instructor, wasn't he?'

'Yes.'

'Probably better that you didn't have anything to do with him.'

'Because of his profession?'

'No, because he accepted being paid off. A parent should never give up a child, no matter what.'

'I'm sorry that happened to you,' she said quietly.

Cruz didn't want her compassion. Especially not when he understood why his mother had done it. Hell, wasn't that one of the reasons he worked so hard? So that if he did ever marry no wife of his would ever have to face the same decision?

He shrugged it off, as he always did. 'I had a lot of opportunities from it. And worse things happen to kids than that.'

'True, but when a child feels abandoned it's—'

He cut off her sympathetic response. 'You move on and you don't look back.'

Aspen registered the pain in his voice, the deep hurt he must have felt. She experienced a strange desire to make him feel better—and then reminded herself that he was a wealthy man who was determined to steal her home away from her and was so arrogant he was lending her money to challenge him.

'I'd like to stop for flowers,' she said stiffly.

Cruz turned down a side street and cursed when the

traffic came to a standstill along a busy ocean-facing bou-
levard, completely oblivious to the cosmopolitan coastline
that sparkled in the sun.

'What?'

'I'd like to stop for flowers.'

'What for?'

She looked pained—and stiff. 'Your mother's birthday,
for one, and the fact that I'm visiting someone's home and
don't have a gift.'

'I told you I have it covered.'

'And given your attitude to money I'm sure it's very
generous, but I would prefer to give something more personal.'

Cruz ground his teeth together, praying for patience.

Five minutes later he swung the big car onto the side of
the road in front of a group of shops. When she made to
get out of the car, he stopped her. 'I'll get them. You wait
here and keep the door locked.'

'But they're supposed to be from me.'

'Believe me, my mother will know who they're from.'
The last time he'd given her flowers he'd picked wild dahl-
ias by the side of the road when he'd been about twelve.

Not long after that Aspen was relieved when Cruz pulled
into the circular driveway of a large *hacienda,* with fat
terracotta pots either side of a wide entrance filled with
colourful blooms.

She stepped out of the car before Cruz reached her side
and saw his scowl grow fiercer as he unloaded a box of
brightly wrapped presents from the back.

'You told me you were giving your mother money,' she
said, confused.

'I am. These are for my nieces and nephews.'

That surprised her, and she wondered if maybe he had
a heart beating somewhere inside his body after all. The

thought lasted for as long as it took for his eager nieces and nephews to descend on him in a wild flurry.

It was as if Santa had arrived and, like that mythical person, Cruz was treated with deference and a little trepidation. As if he wasn't quite real. Aspen saw genuine affection for him on the faces of his family, but it was clear when no one touched or hugged him that all was not quite right between them.

For his part, Cruz didn't seem to notice. His cool gaze was completely tuned in to the delighted squeals of his six nieces and nephews as they unearthed remote-controlled cars, sporting equipment and several dolls. That was when Aspen realised that the gifts were either an ice-breaker or possibly a replacement for any real affection between them.

'This is Aspen,' he said once the furore had died down. 'Aspen, this is my family.'

Succinct, she thought as each one of his family members warily introduced themselves, clearly unsure how to take her. Deciding to ignore the way that made her feel and make the best of the situation, she smiled at them as if there was nothing amiss about her being by Cruz's side.

'These are from both of us,' she said, handing Cruz's mother the elaborate posy he had purchased and watching as her gentle face lit up with pleasure. She must once have been a great beauty, Aspen thought, but time and life had wearied her, lining her face and sprinkling her thick dark hair with silvery streaks. She gazed up at her son with open adoration and Aspen could have kicked Cruz when he barely mustered a stiff smile in return.

An awkward silence fell over his sisters until his brother, Ricardo, took charge and led them all out to the rear patio, where the scent of a heavenly barbecue filled the air.

Cruz's youngest sister, Gabriella, who looked to be about nineteen, hooked her arm through Aspen's and took it upon herself to introduce her two brothers-in-law, who each had a pair of tongs in one hand and a beer in the other.

Gabriella pointed out the small vineyard her mother still tended, and the lush veggie patch in raised wooden boxes. Three well-fed dogs lazed beneath the shade of a lemon-coloured magnolia tree and the view of the ocean from the house was truly spectacular.

'Cruz has never brought a girlfriend here before,' Gabriella whispered.

Aspen smiled enigmatically. She knew the label hadn't come from Cruz but she wasn't about to correct his sister and embarrass them both. And, anyway, 'girlfriend' sounded much better than mistress to her ears, even if it did mean that she had terrible taste in men.

Returning to the patio, she found Cruz sprawled in a deckchair at the head of the large outdoor table, with his sisters and his mother crowded around him like celebrity minders who were worried about losing their jobs. One after the other they asked if he was okay or if he needed anything with embarrassing regularity, offering him food and drink like the Wise Men bestowing gifts on the baby Jesus.

The two brothers-in-law had cleverly retreated to tend the state-of-the-art barbecue, and Aspen tried her best to appreciate the amazing view of grapevines tripping down the hillside towards the azure sea below.

The conversation was like listening to an uninterested child practising the violin: one minute flowing and easy, the next halting and grating. Nobody seemed to know which topic of conversation to stick to.

Even worse, Cruz's mother kept throwing guilty glances his way, while treating him like a king. Cruz either didn't notice, or pretended that he didn't, conversing mainly with his brother about work issues.

It made her think about what Mrs Randall had said the day before. *He missed his family terribly, that boy.*

Ironically, Cruz didn't look as if he had missed them at all, and yet Aspen sensed from his intermittent glances along the table that Mrs Randall had been right.

What had it been like for him? she wondered. On The Farm, all alone and cut off from his family? And how did one reconnect after that?

Bizarrely, she started to feel sorry for him, and found herself wanting to break through the solid barrier he seemed to have erected around himself.

Thankfully one of the older boys brought out the new basketball Cruz had bought and called for everyone to play Four Square. Gabriella jumped up and mercifully asked Aspen to join in. It was the only time Cruz wasn't asked if he wanted to partake.

One of the children quickly drew out four squares and Aspen patiently waited for a cherubic-looking boy with a mop of curly black hair to explain the rules while his ten-year-old sister tapped her foot impatiently and said, 'We know...we *know.*'

Before long there was a mixed line of adults and kids and Aspen found she was enjoying herself for the first time that day, laughing with the children and jockeying for position as king of the game.

When one of the older children tried a shifty manoeuvre the ball went spinning off towards the stone table. Cruz deftly caught it and threw it back to Aspen.

Some devil on Aspen's shoulder made her toss the ball straight back at him. 'Come and play.'

'No, thanks.'

'He never plays games when he comes,' Gabriella whispered.

Aspen gave her a half-smile, knowing exactly how it felt to hanker after the affection of someone who wouldn't give it. She remembered that her grandfather and her uncle had been far too serious to play games with her and she'd very quickly learned not to ask.

Sensing that Cruz was far too serious as well, and that if he just lightened up a little everyone else could start to as well, she bounced the ball back in his direction.

'Are you afraid you'll lose?' she challenged lightly.

He stood up from the table and placed his beer bottle down with deliberate restraint.

Every member of his family seemed to hold their collective breath—even the two men tending the sizzling barbecue—waiting to see what he would do. If a tree had fallen in Africa they would have heard it.

Aspen saw the moment Cruz became conscious of the same thing and the smile on her lips died as he stared at her with a dangerous glint in his eyes. He came towards her slowly, like a hungry panther, his black hair glinting in the sunlight just as she remembered.

A shiver of awareness skittered over her skin. Her mind told her to run, but her body was on another frequency because it remained rooted to the spot.

Towering over her, Cruz took her hand and carefully placed the ball in it, as if he was handing back a newborn baby—or a bomb about to go off. He leant closer, and Aspen forgot about their audience as his gaze shifted to her mouth.

'I said no.'

When his gaze lifted to hers there was an implicit warning for her to behave deep within his cold regard. Then without a word he spun on his heels and stalked towards the garden.

Aspen released a shaky breath and heard Gabriella do the same.

'Doesn't he scare you when he frowns at you like that?'

His sister was right. His anger should have scared her. Terrified her, in fact. Her grandfather had wielded his temper like a weapon and when Chad had been drunk he had been volatile and moody. But Cruz didn't scare her in that way. Other ways, yes. Like the way he made her feel shivery and out of control of her senses. As if when he touched her he consumed her, controlled her.

That scared her.

Pushing her troubled thoughts aside, she sought to reassure Gabriella. 'No, he doesn't scare me that way. I think his bark—or his look—is more ferocious than his bite.'

The sound of the back door opening drew Aspen's gaze from Cruz's retreating figure and she watched Ricardo back out of the doorway, an elaborate birthday cake resplendent with pink icing and brightly coloured flowers held gingerly in his arms.

'Where's Cruz?' he asked, casting a quick glance at the now vacant chair.

There was a bit of low murmuring that Aspen understood, despite not speaking Spanish, and she felt a guilty flush highlight her cheekbones. It was her fault that Cruz had stalked off.

'I'll go and get him.'

Ricardo looked as if he was about to argue with her but then changed his mind. 'Thank you.'

Following the path Cruz had taken, she found him out by the small vineyard, his head bent towards a leafy vine laden with bunches of purple grapes. The bright sun darkened his olive skin as he stood there, which was extremely unfair, Aspen thought, when her skin was more likely to turn pink and blister.

A bee buzzed lazily past her face and she stepped out of its way.

Cruz must have heard the sound of her steps on the dirt

but he gave no indication of it, putting his hands in his pockets and staring out across the ocean like a god from the days of old. Strong. Formidable. *Impenetrable.*

'I was hoping for a moment's peace,' he said without turning around, his deep voice a master of creation.

'They're about to serve the birthday cake,' Aspen informed him softly.

'So they sent you to find me?'

'No.' She stood beside him and watched tiny waves break further out to sea. 'I volunteered.'

He made a noise that seemed to say she was an idiot. And she was—because she had an overpowering urge to reach out to him.

'They don't know how to treat you, you know.' She glanced up at him, no longer able to ignore what had been going on since they arrived. 'Your mother seems to be suffering. From guilt? Remorse? It's not clear, but it *is* clear that she loves you. They all do.'

Cruz tensed and dug his hands further into his pockets. Aspen had inadvertently picked a scab off an old wound. He knew his mother felt guilty. He'd told her she shouldn't but it hadn't worked. He had no idea what to do about that and it made being around his family almost impossible, because he knew that without him around they would be up singing and dancing and having a great time.

'Don't start talking about what you can't possibly understand,' he grated harshly.

'I understand that you're upset…maybe a little angry about what happened to you,' she offered gently.

He swung around to face her. 'I'm not angry about that. When my father died it was my job as the eldest boy to take care of my family while the girls ran the house. It's what we did. Rallied around each other and banded together.'

'Oh, dear, that must have made it even harder for you to leave them.'

Cruz scowled down at her. 'It's not like I had a say in it. Old Man Carmichael offered my mother money and she preferred to send me away than to let me provide for the family my way.'

'Which was…?'

Mostly he'd worked at a nearby *hacienda* and tended rich people's gardens. Sometimes he'd done odd jobs for the men his father had become involved with, but he hadn't been stupid enough to do anything illegal. Anything criminal.

'Boring stuff.'

'And your mother didn't work herself?'

'She cleaned houses when she could, but I have one brother and four sisters. All were under ten at the time. My father's family were what you would politely term dysfunctional, and my mother had been an only child to elderly parents. If I hadn't stepped up, nobody else would have.'

'I'm sorry, Cruz. That's a lot for a child to have heaped on his shoulders. You must have really struggled.' She grimaced. 'I guess that's why they treat you like you're a king now.'

He looked at her sharply. 'They don't treat me like a king. They act like it didn't happen. They tiptoe around me as if I'm about to go off at them.'

She paused and Cruz caught the concern in her gaze. Something tightened in his chest. What was he doing, spilling his childhood stories to this woman? A person he didn't even *like*.

As if sensing his volatile thoughts she murmured half to herself and he had to strain to capture the words. '…not real.'

'Excuse me?' He glanced at her sharply. 'Are you saying my feelings for my family are not real?'

'Of course not. Though it might help them relax a bit if you scowled a little less.' She shot him a half-smile. 'I can see that you love your family. Which is strangely reassuring though I don't know why. But there's no hugging. No touching.' Her pause was laden with unwanted empathy. 'Truthfully, you remind me of my grandfather. He found it tough to let anyone get close to him as well.'

His eyes narrowed. Nobody in his family talked about the past—not even Ricardo. Cruz had come back from Ocean Haven eight years ago angry—yes, by God, *angry*—and he'd stayed that way. And he liked it. Anger drove him and defined him. Made him hungry and kept him on his guard.

He looked at Aspen. Unfortunately for her he was *really* angry now. 'I don't remember reading anywhere in that makeshift document of yours that pop psychology was part of our deal.'

Her eyes flashed up at him. 'I was only trying to help. Though I don't know why,' she muttered, half under her breath, inflaming his anger even more.

'Helping wasn't part of it either. There's only one thing I want from you. Conversation before or after is not only superfluous, it's irrelevant.'

She gave him that hurt look again, before masking it with cool hauteur, and he felt his teeth grind together.

Dammit, why couldn't he look at her without feeling so…so *much*?

All the time.

Lust, anger, disappointment, hunger. A deep hunger for more—and not just of that sweet body which had haunted more dreams than he cared to remember.

He reminded himself of the type of woman she was. The type who would use that body to further her own interests.

She'd used it to good effect to deceive him years ago and hadn't cared a damn for his feelings. That was real. That was who she was. And once he'd had her in his bed, had slaked his lust for her—*used* her in return—then she'd be out of his life and his head.

Hell, he couldn't wait.

CHAPTER SIX

IT WAS EARLY evening by the time Cruz turned onto the long stretch of driveway that led to the Rodriquez Polo Club. A hotel, Aspen had heard it said, that was a hotel to end all hotels.

She didn't care. She was too keyed-up to be impressed. And, anyway, it was just a hotel.

Only it wasn't *just* anything. It was magnificent.

A palatial honey-coloured building that looked about ten storeys high, it curved like a giant horseshoe around a network of manicured gardens with a central fountain that resembled an inverted chandelier.

As soon as their SUV stopped a uniformed concierge jumped to attention and treated Cruz with the deference one usually expected only around royalty.

Expensively clad men and women wandered languidly in and out of the glassed entrance as if all their cares in the world had disappeared and Aspen glanced down at her old top and jeans. Despite the fact that her grandfather had once been seriously wealthy, Ocean Haven hadn't done well for so long that Aspen couldn't remember the last personal item she'd bought other than deodorant. Now she felt like Cinderella *before* the makeover, and it only seemed to widen the gulf between her and the brooding man beside her.

'Well, I can see why it's rated as seven stars and I

haven't even seen inside yet,' she said with reluctant admiration. 'And, oh…wow…' she added softly. A row of bronzed life-sized horses that looked as if they were racing each other in a shallow pool with shots of water trickling around them glowed under strategically placed lights, adding both pizazz and majesty to the entrance. 'There's so much to see. I almost don't want to go inside.'

'Unfortunately we're not allowed to serve meals on the kerb so you'll have to.'

Aspen switched her gaze to Cruz at his unexpected humour and her pulse skittered. He was just so handsome and charismatic. What would it feel like, she wondered, to be with him at the hotel because she *wanted* to be there and he *wanted* her to be there with him?

The unexpected thought had her nearly stumbling over her own feet.

Why was she even thinking like that?

The last thing she needed was to become involved with a man again. And Cruz had told her in no uncertain terms that he expected sex and nothing else. No need to pretty it up with unwanted emotion.

How had she convinced herself that she'd be able to do this? Not only because of her own inherent dislike of sex but because it was so cold. What would happen once they got upstairs? Did they go straight to the bedroom? Undress? Would he undress her? No. Probably not.

Fortunately she didn't have much time to contemplate the sick feeling in the pit of her stomach as the doorman swept open the chrome and glass doors and inclined his head as Cruz strode inside. Aspen scurried to keep up and couldn't help but notice the lingering attention Cruz garnered with effortless ease.

Another deferential staff member in a severely cut suit descended on him and Aspen left them to stroll towards a circular platform with a large wood carving of a polo player on horseback.

'Aspen?'

Having finished up with his employee, Cruz waited impatiently for her to come to him but Aspen couldn't help returning her gaze to the intricate carving.

'Did you do this?'

He looked startled. 'Why would you think that?'

'I just saw some smaller versions in your mother's house and they reminded me of the wood carvings you used to do in your spare time. Were they yours?'

He paused and Aspen felt a little foolish.

'I haven't done one of those in years.'

It was the most he'd said to her since leaving his mother's and her curiosity got the better of her. 'You don't play polo any more either. Why is that?'

For a minute she didn't think he had heard her.

'Other things to do.'

'Do you miss it?' she asked, imagining that he couldn't not, considering how good he was.

'Mind your step when you come down,' he said, turning away from her.

Right. That would be the end of yet another conversation, she thought, wondering why she'd even bothered to try and engage him. Her natural curiosity and desire to help others was clearly wasted on this man.

She thought back to his angry response to her gentle prodding at his mother's house and shook her head at her own gumption. What did she really know, anyway? Her own relationship history wasn't exactly the healthiest on the planet.

Following Cruz to the bank of elevators, she decided to keep her mouth shut. It was hard enough contemplating what she was about to do without adding to it by trying to come up with superfluous conversation.

When the lift opened directly into Cruz's private suite Aspen gasped at the opulence of the living area, but Cruz ignored it all, striding into the room and throwing his wallet and keys onto a large mahogany table with an elaborate floral arrangement in the centre. With barely a pause he pushed open a set of concertina glass doors that led to a long balcony. Beyond the doors Aspen could just make out a jewel-green polo field.

Stepping closer, she saw that beyond the field there was an enormous stone stable with an orange tiled roof and beyond that white-fenced paddocks holding, she knew, some of the finest polo ponies in the world.

'Wow....' She breathed hot evening air that carried the scent of freshly mown grass and the lemony scent of magnolia with it. 'Is that a swimming pool out there to the right?'

'Yes.' Cruz had his hands wedged firmly in his pockets as he stood behind her. 'It's a saltwater pool the horses use to cool off in.'

'Lucky horses.'

'If you take ten steps to your left and look around the corner you'll see a pool and spa *you* can use.'

Happy to move out of his commanding orbit, Aspen followed his directions.

'Oh...' She stared at a sapphire-blue lap pool which had a large spa at the end of it. The pool was shielded on one side by a thick hedge and from above by a strategically placed cloth sail that would block both the sun and any paparazzi snooping around. 'You don't do things by halves, do you?'

'Mexico is a hot place.'

Then why did she feel so cold?

Shivering, she glanced back at him, her attention caught by piercing black eyes and the dark stubble that highlighted his square jaw. Those broad shoulders...

She shivered again, and tossed her head to cover her reaction. 'Time to get this party started, I'd say.'

'Party?' He raised a cool eyebrow at her. 'In the pool?'

Aspen cast a quick glance at the inviting water, alarmed as an image of both of them naked and entwined popped into her head. It was so clear she could almost see them there—his larger, tanned body holding her up, the silky feel of the water lapping at her skin as it rippled with their movements, her arms curved over his smooth shoulders as she steadied herself, his hands stroking her heavy breasts....

She felt her face flame. She had the romantic—the *fantasy*—version of sex in her mind. The real version, she knew from experience, could never live up to it.

'Of course not.'

'Have you ever made love in the water, Aspen?'

Had he moved closer to her? She glanced at him with alarm but he hadn't moved. Or hadn't appeared to.

She inhaled and steeled her spine. 'The pool doesn't appeal to me.'

'Pity. It's a nice night for it.'

Aspen didn't want to complicate this. A bed was more than adequate for what was about to happen between them. And she could close her eyes more easily in a bed.

'A bed is fine.'

She wondered if Cruz would put a towel down, the way Chad had done.

A muscle ticked in Cruz's jaw and he stared at her as if trying to discern all her deepest thoughts. Then he turned abruptly away. 'Actually, I find I don't enjoy making love on an empty stomach.'

'This has nothing to do with love,' Aspen reminded him assertively.

Halfway to returning indoors, Cruz stopped and his

black eyes smouldered. 'When I touch your body, Aspen, you'll think it does.'

Oh, how arrogant was *that*? If only he knew that all his Latin charm was wasted on her.

Aspen hurled mental daggers at his broad back and wondered why he didn't want to get this over with as soon as possible. By all accounts he seemed to want her—but then so had Chad in the beginning. Oh, this was beyond awful. She hated second-guessing Cruz's desire. Hated hoping that with him it would be different. She knew better than to count on hope. It hadn't brought her mother or her father back into her life. It hadn't made her grandfather love her for herself in the end.

This time when she looked around the vast living area she noticed a bottle of champagne in a silver ice bucket on the main dining table. Maybe that was what she should do. Get drunk.

As if reading her mind, Cruz tightened his mouth. 'Come—I'll show you to your room.'

Aspen felt her heart bump inside her chest. *He's just showing you the room, you fool, not asking you to use it.*

Yet.

Standing back to let her pass, Cruz indicated towards a closed door. 'The bathroom, which should be stocked with everything you'll need, is through there.'

Aspen nodded, feeling completely overwhelmed.

When it became obvious she wasn't going to say anything Cruz turned to go. 'I'll leave you to freshen up.'

She noticed a book on the bedside table. 'This is your room,' she blurted out.

'You were expecting someone else's?'

'No. I...' She spared him a tart look. 'I thought you might like your own space.'

'I like my bed warm more.'

Right.

'Dinner should be served in twenty minutes.'

After he closed the door behind him Aspen sagged against the silk-covered king bed and wondered how long it would be before he realised she was a dud.

Feeling completely despondent, she picked up the novel beside the bed and noticed it was one of her favourites. Surprised, she flicked through it. Could he really be reading it or was it just for show? Just to impress the plethora of mistresses who wandered in and out of his life?

An hour later she was wound so tight all she could do was pick at the delicious Mexican dinner that for once didn't include *tacos* and *enchiladas*.

'Something wrong?'

Her eyes slid across Cruz's powerful forearms, exposed by his rolled shirtsleeves.

Was he serious? She was about to embarrass herself with a man who didn't even like her in order to save her home. Of *course* there was something wrong.

'Of course not,' she replied, feigning relaxed confidence.

He frowned down at her plate. 'Is it the *birria*? If it's too hot for you I can order something else.'

Oh, he'd meant the food. 'No, no, the food's lovely.'

He put down his fork and brought his wine glass to his lips. Now, *there* was relaxed confidence, she thought a little resentfully.

'Then why is most of it still on your plate?'

He licked a drop of red wine from his lower lip and Aspen couldn't look away. Remembered pleasure at the way his mouth had taken hers in the most wonderful kiss vied with sheer terror for supremacy. Unfortunately sheer terror was winning out, because he looked like a man who would expect everything and the kitchen sink as well.

'I…um…I ate a lot at the party.'

'No, you didn't. You barely touched a thing.'

'I'm not a big eater at the best of times.'

'And these are far from the best of times—is that it, Aspen?'

It was more of a statement than a question and Aspen wondered if perhaps he felt the same way. 'You could say that,' she said carefully.

'Is that because you're still in love with Anderson?'

'Sorry?' She knew her mouth was hanging open and she snapped it closed. '*No.* No, that was a disaster from the start.'

'So you're not still pining for him?'

'No.'

His eyes narrowed thoughtfully. 'Why was it a disaster?'

Had she really just told him being married to Chad had been a disaster? 'Don't ask.'

'I just did.'

'Yes, well, I'd rather not talk about it, if it's all the same to you.'

He sat staring at her and Aspen wished she knew what to say next. His unexpected question about Chad had completely derailed her.

'Come here.'

The soft command made her senses leap and she felt her breath quicken with rising panic. He was trying to control her, and she knew she couldn't let him do that.

She tossed her hair back behind one shoulder. 'You come here.'

Despite the fact that he hadn't moved she could sense the tightly coiled tension within him. It radiated outward across the table and stole the breath from her lungs. And for all her dismissive tone she still felt like a puppet on his string—despite her resolve not to be.

He watched her with heavy-lidded eyes and she was

totally unprepared for the scrape of his chair on the terracotta tiles as he stood up.

Aspen's heart jumped as if she'd been startled out of a trance.

Determined to remain neutral—outwardly at least—she didn't move. Couldn't, if the truth be told. Her limbs were completely paralysed—by his laconic sensuality as much as her own blinding insecurities.

'You have amazing hair.'

She snatched in a quick breath to feed her starving lungs. She could feel the heat emanating from his strong thighs beside her shoulders and even though he hadn't touched her she started to tremble. Her only saving grace was that he couldn't possibly be aware of her inner turmoil, and she stared straight ahead as she felt him roll a strand of her hair between his fingers as if it were the finest silk.

She couldn't do this. Already she was freezing up, and to put herself at another man's mercy was truly frightening.

Chad's roughness crowded her mind and permeated her soul, and it was as if Cruz ceased to exist in that moment.

'Dammit, Aspen. What is wrong with you?'

Cruz's dark, annoyed voice only added fuel to the raging fire of Aspen's insecurities. Panic enveloped her and galvanised her into action.

Gouging the floor tiles with her chair, she forced it back and moved in the opposite direction from the one Cruz was in. Unfortunately that only brought her to the balustrade. She gripped the iron railing, enjoying the coolness of the metal against her overheated palms, and pretended rapt attention in the glowing lights that outlined the low boards around the darkened polo field.

'What bothers you the most about this?' he grated. 'The money aspect or the fact that it's me you'll be sleeping with?'

Aspen knew he stood close behind her—every fibre of

her being felt as if it was attuned to every fibre of his—but she didn't turn around. Honestly, she should have known that when it came to the crunch she would fall at the first hurdle. But of course she needed to do this—her mind was so fogged that she couldn't comprehend any other way to save her farm.

'It's not the money.' She tilted her gaze to take in the starry sky. She was planning to pay him back every cent he loaned her, plus interest, so she'd reconciled that in her mind before he'd even picked her up. No, it was… 'It's—'

'Me?' The single word sounded like a pistol-shot.

Interesting, she thought, holding a conversation with someone you couldn't see. It made her other senses come alive. Her sense of hearing that was so in love with the deep timbre of his voice, the feel of the heat of his body that seemed to reach out like a beckoning light, his smell… Unconsciously she rubbed at the railing and felt the smooth texture of the iron beneath her sensitive fingertips.

'It's more the fact that you don't like me,' she said on a rush.

She hadn't realised how true that was until the words left her mouth. A beat passed and then she felt his hands on her shoulders, gently turning her. Embarrassed by the admission, she forced herself to meet his gaze. Because she knew she was right.

He stared at her, not saying anything, his large hands burning into the tops of her shoulders, his thumbs almost absently caressing her collarbones. It was hard to read his expression with only a candle flickering on the table and a crescent moon ducking behind darkened clouds. It was even harder when he lowered his gaze to his hands, his inky lashes shielding them.

He gently slid those large hands up her neck to the line of her jaw, setting off a whole host of sensations in their wake. Aspen stiffened as she felt the pad of one of his thumbs slowly graze her closed mouth. His eyes locked on her lips as he pressed into the soft flesh, making them feel gloriously sensitised.

They were both utterly still. The only movement came from his thumb as it swept back and forth, back and forth, across her hyper-sensitive flesh. Back and forth until her lips started to buzz and gave beneath the persuasive pressure, allowing him to reach the moisture within. Aspen trembled as he spread her own wetness along her bottom lip and then opened her lips wider, until he was touching her teeth. He traced their shape just as thoroughly, only they weren't as malleable as her lips and stayed firmly closed.

She should have known that he wouldn't stop there. Unfairly he was bringing his fingers into play, to knead the side of her neck, pressing firmly into her nape. On a rush of heat her senses were overloaded and her teeth parted, giving him greater liberties.

Only he didn't immediately take them, and without even realising it Aspen tilted her head, seeking to capture his thumb between her teeth, silently inviting him inside. Still he hung back, and with a small sound in the back of her throat she couldn't stop her mouth from closing around his thumb and sucking on his flesh, couldn't stop her tongue from wrapping itself around it as she sought to taste him.

Cruz didn't know if he'd ever experienced anything as erotic as Aspen drawing his thumb into her wide mouth, her cheeks hollowing as she sucked firmly and then softening as she used her tongue to drive him wild. With every stroke his erection jerked painfully behind his zipper and, unable to hold back any longer, he pulled his thumb from her mouth and replaced it with his own.

She immediately latched onto his mouth as if she was just as desperate as he was, and he backed her against the cast iron balustrading and didn't stop until he was hard up against her.

Incapable of thought, he let his instincts take over and hooked one of her legs up over his hip so he could settle into the cradle of her thighs, all the time ravaging her mouth until she fed him more of those hot little moans.

The deep neckline of her otherwise demure dress, which had tantalised him all night, was no barrier to his wandering hands and he deftly moved the soft jersey aside and cupped her, squeezing her full breasts together. He strummed his thumbs over her lace-covered nipples and felt exalted when she arched into him, moaning more keenly as he slowly increased the pressure.

He groaned, licked his way to her ear, bit it, and then trailed tiny kisses down over her neck, sucking on her soft skin. She smelled like flowers and tasted like honey and he knew he'd never experienced anything so sweet. So heady.

Her leg shifted higher as she sought a deeper contact, and her fingers dug into his shoulders as if she was trying to hold herself upright.

'Cruz, please.…'

Needing no further invitation, he pushed her bra aside and leant back so that he could look at her.

'Perfect. You fit perfectly into my hands.'

He moulded her fullness, watching her beautiful raspberry-coloured nipples tighten even more as they anticipated his mouth on them. His body throbbed as it anticipated the same thing, and he tested the weight of each breast before drawing his thumb and fingertips together until he held just the tips of each nipple between his fingers, his touch too light to fully satisfy.

She cried out and arched impossibly higher, as if in pain, and he bent his head and gave her what he knew she needed, soldering his lips to one peak and pulling her turgid flesh deeply into his mouth while rubbing firmly over the other.

'Cruz! Oh, my God!'

She buried her hands in his hair and clung—and thank goodness she did. The taste of her made his knees feel weak and his hunger to be buried deep inside her impossibly urgent.

Wrapping one arm around her waist, he lifted her and ground his hardness against her core, his self-control shredded by her wild response. 'I want you, Aspen.' He smoothed his hand down the silky skin of her thigh and rode her skirt all the way up. 'Tell me you want me, *mi gatita*. Tell me this has nothing to do with money.'

He registered the rigidity in her body at the same time as his rough words reverberated inside his head, and both acted like a bucket of cold water on his libido.

What was he saying? More importantly, what was he *asking*?

'I...'

She looked up at him, flushed with passion. Dazed. Beautiful. The breeze whispered over her hair.

'I'm sorry,' she whispered breathlessly.

Sorry?

So was he.

The last time he had wanted something this badly he had lost everything. And he couldn't take her like this.

Couldn't take her because he was paying her.

Once again the image of a lustful Billy Smyth with his hand stroking her face clouded his vision. Up to yesterday Cruz would have said that he wasn't a violent man, but just the thought of her sleeping with anyone else curdled his blood. If he hadn't offered her this deal where else might she be tonight—and who with?

The question just added ice to the bucket and he unwound her arms from around his neck.

'Cruz...?'

Was he crazy? He had a hot woman in his arms so why was he hesitating? He couldn't explain it; he just knew it didn't feel right.

His hard-on pressed insistently against his fly, as if to say it had felt very right ten seconds ago, and he stepped away from her so he wouldn't be tempted to pull her back into his arms.

Something of his inner turmoil must have shown on his face, because she blanched and he thought she might throw up.

'Steady.'

He went to grab her but she pulled back sharply and quickly righted her dress as best she could before wrapping her arms around herself.

'I can't believe it. I've ruined it,' she muttered, more to herself than him.

On one level he registered the comment as strange, but part of him had already agreed with her—because, yes, she *had* ruined it. She was ruining everything.

His desire to buy Ocean Haven.

His peace of mind.

'That sounds like revenge,' she'd said earlier.

'Go to bed, Aspen,' he said wearily, upset with himself and his unwelcome conscience.

Her eyes were uncertain pools of dark green when she looked at him. 'But what about—?'

'I'm not in the mood.'

He turned sharply and tracked back into the penthouse before he threw his aggravating conscience over the balcony and did what his body was all but demanding he do.

Aspen stood on the balcony, the night air cooling her over-heated skin as the realisation that he was rejecting her sank in. She swallowed heavily, her mind spinning back to those last few moments. She felt like an inept fool as memories of Chad's hurtful rejection of her years ago tumbled into her mind like an avalanche. His repulsed expression when he'd told her to go out and buy a bottle of lube.

At the time she'd been so naïve about sex she hadn't even known what he was talking about. So he'd clarified. *'Lubrication. You're too dry. It's off-putting.'*

Completely mortified, she'd searched the internet and learned that some women suffered dryness due to low oestrogen levels. She hadn't investigated any further. She'd shame-facedly done what he'd asked, but they'd never got round to using it. He hadn't wanted to touch her after that.

And no matter how many times she told herself that Chad's harsh words were more to do with his own inadequacies in the bedroom than hers it didn't matter. She didn't believe it. Not entirely. There was always a niggle that he was right.

Don't go there, she warned herself, only half aware that she had pressed her hand to her stomach. *Chad's long gone and you knew this was going to happen with Cruz so, okay, deal with it. And quickly. Then you can go home to Ocean Haven and be safe again.*

Fortifying her resolve, she moved inside and found Cruz pouring a drink, his back to her.

'You still have to lend me the money,' she said, glad that her voice sounded so strong.

Cruz felt his shoulders tense and turned slowly to face her.

She was a cool one, all right. Haughty. Dismissive. *Way too good for him.*

Slowly he folded himself into one of the deep-seated sofas. 'No, I don't,' he said, wanting to annoy her.

'Yes, you do. You signed—'

'I know what I signed.' He swirled his drink and ice clinked in the glass as he watched her. Her eyes were cool to the point of being detached. Damn her. That was usually *his* stock in trade.

'Then you know that if it turns out you don't want...' She stopped whatever it was she was about to say and raised her chin. 'I trusted you.'

He ignored the way those words twisted his gut. Her soft declaration was making his conscience spike again. 'The agreement didn't stipulate which night.' He waited for his words to sink in and it didn't take long. 'Consider yourself off the hook for tonight. As I told you, I'm not in the mood.'

She frowned. 'When *will* you be in the mood?'

Right now, as it happens.

'I don't know,' he said roughly, annoyed with his inability to control his physical response to her.

Of course that answer wasn't good enough for her.

'And if *I'm* not in the mood when you decide you are?'

This wasn't going to work. If he stayed here he'd damned well finish what he had started outside.

He sprang to his feet and those green eyes widened warily. And well they might. He stalked towards her and wrapped one hand around that glorious mane of hair. He tilted her face up so that she was forced to meet his steely gaze, unsure if he was angry with her or himself or just in general.

'When I decide to take you, Aspen, rest assured you'll be in the mood.'

Then he kissed her. Long and deep and hard.

Aspen held the back of her hand against her throbbing mouth as Cruz marched out through the main door to the lift.

And good riddance, she wanted to call out to his arrogant back. Except she didn't. She felt too shattered. Lack of sleep last night, the roller coaster of a day today. It all crashed in on her.

Not wanting to wait around in case he suddenly reappeared, she fled to the bedroom, hoping sleep would transport her back to East Hampton. Literally.

Only it wasn't her room she was in, and she quickly snatched her things together and headed to one of the spare bedrooms.

Ha—she would show him who wasn't 'in the mood'.

She let out a low groan as those words he had flung at her came rushing back. The embarrassing thing was she couldn't have been more in the mood if he had lit scented candles and told her he loved her.

And he had seemed to be totally in the mood.

When she found herself trying to analyse the exact moment it had all gone wrong she pulled herself up. That was a one-way street to anxiety and sleeplessness and she wouldn't go there again. Not for any man.

By the time Cruz let himself back into the penthouse his frame of mind had not improved. He'd gone down to the stables—something he'd always done when he felt troubled—but it hadn't made him feel any better.

In fact it had made him feel worse, because now that Aspen had walked back into his life—or rather he had walked back into hers—he couldn't get her out of his head.

Worse, he couldn't get the game he was playing with her out of his head. He'd had a lot of time to think about things since he'd picked her up, and although he'd like to be able to say that it had started out as an underhand way of getting what he wanted the truth was it hadn't even been that logical. He'd taken one look at her and wanted her. Then he'd made the mistake of touching her. Kissing her. He'd never felt so out of control. Something he hadn't anticipated at all.

He'd convinced himself that he could sleep with her for one night and send her home.

So much for that.

The reality was that right now he wanted her in his bed—and not because he was paying her a pit full of money but because she wanted to be there. And didn't that make his head spin? The last time he'd wanted something from a Carmichael he'd been kicked in the teeth, and he was about as likely to let that happen again as the sun rising in the west.

He thought about her comment about his family treating him like a king. He'd been so caught up in his own sense of betrayal and, yes, his anger at missing out on *knowing* them that he hadn't considered his own involvement in continuing that state of affairs. Now he saw it through Aspen's eyes and it made him want to cringe. Yes, he held himself back. But distance made things easier to manage.

But she had understood that as well, hadn't she? *'That's a lot for a child to have heaped on his shoulders. You must have really struggled.'*

Yes, it had been a lot. Particularly when Charles Carmichael had been such an exacting and forbidding taskmaster. Maybe others understood what he had gone through but no one had dared say it to his face.

And her suggestion that he could scowl a little less…?

He scowled now. Maybe he should just go and find her, have sex with her and be done with her. But something about that snagged in his unconscious. Something wasn't right about her hot and cold responses but he couldn't put his finger on what it was.

'I can't believe it. I've ruined it.'

Why would she have said that? If anything he'd ruined it by stopping. But she hadn't questioned that, had she? She'd had a look on her face that was one of resigned acceptance and moved on.

And hard on the heels of that thought was her comment about her marriage to Anderson being a disaster. He'd wanted to push her on that but had decided not to. Now he wished he had. There was something about the lack of defiance in her eyes when she had mentioned her ex that bothered him. Almost as if she'd been terribly hurt by the whole thing.

He frowned. The truth was he shouldn't give a damn about Aspen Carmichael, or her feelings, or her comments, and he didn't know why he did.

Throwing off his tangled thoughts, he tentatively pushed open his bedroom door and stopped short when he found the room empty. His wardrobe door lay open and a stream of feminine clothing crossed his room like a trail of breadcrumbs where she had obviously dropped them as she'd carried her things out.

Gingerly he picked them up and placed them on the corner chair. She'd no doubt be upset to realise she'd dropped them. Especially the silky peach-coloured panties. He rubbed the fabric between his thumb and forefinger and his body reacted like a devoted dog that had just seen its master return after a year-long absence.

'Not tonight, Josephine,' he muttered, heading for the shower.

A cold one.

Cruz rubbed his rough jaw and picked up his razor. Unbidden, Charles Carmichael's rangy features came to his mind. Initially he had admired his determination and objectivity. His loyalty. Only those traits hadn't stacked up in the end. The man had been ruthless more than determined, cold rather than objective, and his loyalty had been prejudiced towards his own kind.

Had *he* degenerated into that person? Had *he* become a hollow version of the man he'd thought he was? He stopped shaving and stared at the remaining cream on his face. Why did his life suddenly feel so empty? So superficial?

Hold on. His life wasn't empty or superficial. He barked out a short laugh. He had everything a man could want. Money. Power. Women. Respect.

His razor nicked the delicate skin just under his jaw.

Respect.

He didn't have everyone's respect. He didn't have Aspen's. And he didn't have his own right now, either.

He thought again about the night Aspen had set him up. He supposed he could have defended himself against Carmichael's prejudiced accusations and changed the course of his life, but something in Aspen's eyes that night had stayed him. Fear? Devastation? Embarrassment? He'd never asked. He'd just felt angry and bitter that she had stolen his future.

Only she hadn't, had she? He'd disowned it. He'd thrown it all in. Nobody made a fool of a Rodriguez—wasn't that what his *padre* would have said?

He took a deep steadying breath, flexed his shoulders and heard his neck crack back into place.

So, okay, in the morning he would tell Aspen to go home. He wouldn't sleep with her in exchange for the money. She could have it. But she still wasn't getting The Farm. He wanted it, and what he wanted he got.

End of story.

CHAPTER SEVEN

WHEN SHE WOKE the next morning and decided she really couldn't hang out in her room all day Aspen ventured out into the living area of Cruz's luxury penthouse and breathed a sigh of relief to find it empty. Empty bar the lingering traces of his mouth-watering aftershave, that was.

After making sure that he really had gone she sucked in a grateful breath, so on edge she nearly jumped out of her skin when the phone in her hand buzzed with an incoming text.

Make yourself comfortable and charge whatever you want to the room. We'll talk tonight.

'About a ticket home?' she mused aloud.

The disaster of the previous night winged into her thoughts like a homing pigeon.

In the back of her mind Aspen had imagined that they would try to have sex, she would freeze, Cruz might or might not laugh, and Aspen would return home. Then she would get on with her life and never think of him again.

Only nothing was normal with Cruz. Not her inability to hate him for his ruthlessness or her physical reaction to him. Because while she had been in his arms last night she had forgotten to be worried. She'd been unable to do anything but feel, and his touch had felt amazing. So amazing that she'd mistakenly believed it might work. That this time she would be okay. Then she'd panicked and he'd stopped. And she really didn't want to analyse why that was.

'Urgh.' She blew out a breath. 'You weren't going to replay that train wreck again, remember?'

Right.

Determinedly she dropped her phone into her handbag and poured herself a steaming cup of coffee from the silver tray set on the mahogany dining table.

There was an array of gleaming dome-covered plates, and as she lifted each one in turn she wondered if Cruz had ordered the entire menu for breakfast and then realised that he wasn't hungry. Her own stomach signalled that she was ravenous and Aspen placed scrambled eggs and bacon on a plate and tucked in.

Unsure what do with herself, she checked in with Donny and Mrs Randall and then decided to do some studying. She was doing a double load at university next semester, so she could qualify by the end of the year, and she needed to get her head around the coursework before assignments started rolling in.

But she couldn't concentrate.

A horse whinnied in the distance and another answered.

The call of the wild, she mused with a faint smile. She walked out onto the balcony and leant on the railing. The grooms in the distance were leading a group of horses through their morning exercises and the sight made her feel homesick.

It was probably a mistake to go looking for her, but after three hours locked in a business meeting with his executive team, who had flown in from all over the States for a strategy session, Cruz's brain was fried. Distracted by a curly-haired blonde. He told his team to take an early lunch, because he knew better than to push something when it wasn't working. Once he'd found Aspen and organised for her to return to Ocean Haven he'd be able to think again. Until then at least the members of his team could find something more productive to do than repeat every point back to him for the rest of the day.

But, annoyingly, Aspen wasn't anywhere he had expected her to be. Not in his penthouse, nor the hotel boutiques, not one of the five hotel restaurants, nor the day spa. When he described her to his staff they all looked at him as if he was describing some fantasy woman.

Yeah, your fantasy woman.

Feeling more and more agitated, he stopped by the concierge's desk in case she had taken a taxi into town on her own. It would be just like her to do something monumentally stupid and cause him even more problems. Of course the concierge on duty knew immediately who he was talking about and that just turned his mood blacker.

'The strawberry blonde babe with the pre-Raphaelite curls all the way down to her—?'

'Yes, that one,' Cruz snapped, realising that someone—him—had neglected to inform his staff that she was off-limits.

Oblivious to his mounting tension, the concierge continued blithely, 'She's in the stables. At least she was a couple of hours ago.'

And how, he wanted to ask the hapless youth, *do you know that?* His mind conjured up all sorts of clandestine meetings between her and his college-age employee.

Growling under his breath, Cruz stalked across the wide expanse of green lawn that had nothing on her eyes towards the main stable. He reminded himself that if he'd waited around for her to wake up he would now know where she was and what she was up to.

Survival tactics? his conscience proposed.

Busy, Cruz amended.

He heard the lovely sound of her laughter before he saw her, and then the sight of her long legs encased in snug jeans came into view. He couldn't see the rest of her; bent as she was over the stall door, but frankly he couldn't take his eyes off her wiggling hips and the mouthwatering curve of her backside.

Another giggle brought his eyes up and he had to clear his throat twice before she reared back and stood in front of him. Cruz glanced inside the stall in time to see one of his men stuffing his wallet into his back pocket, a guilty flush suffusing his neck.

Unused to such testy feelings of jealousy, and on the verge of grabbing his very married assistant trainer by the throat and hauling him off the premises, Cruz clenched his jaw. 'I believe your services are required elsewhere, Señor Martin.'

'Of course, sir.' His trainer swallowed hard as he opened the stall door and ducked around Aspen. 'Excuse me, *señorita*.'

'Oh, we were just—' Aspen stopped speaking as Luis turned worried eyes her way, and she glanced at Cruz to find his icy stare on the man. He might have been wearing another expensive suit, but he looked anything but civilised, she noted. In fact he looked breathtakingly *un*-civilised—as if he had a band of warriors waiting outside to raid the place.

Irritated both by his overbearing attitude and the way her heart did a little dance behind her breastbone at the sight of him, Aspen went on the attack. 'Don't tell me.' She arched a brow. 'You've suddenly decided you're in the mood?'

'No.'

His expression grew stormier and he stepped into her space until Aspen found herself inside the stall with the almost sleeping horse Luis had been tending to.

'What are you up to, Aspen?' he rasped harshly, blocking the doorway.

Wanting to put space between them, Aspen stepped lightly around the mare and picked up the discarded brush Luis had been using to groom her.

'I feel bad that Luis didn't get to finish in here because of our conversation so I thought I'd brush Bandit down for him.'

'I meant *with* him?'

She paused, not liking the tone of his voice. 'If you're implying what I think you are then, yes, I did offer to sleep with Luis—but unfortunately he only has a spare nine million lying around.' She shrugged as if to say, *What can you do?*

'Don't be smart.'

Aspen glared at him. 'Then don't be insulting.'

He looked at her as if he was contemplating throttling her, but even that wasn't enough to stop the thrilling buzz coursing through her body at his closeness.

Aspen shook her head as much at herself as him. 'You really have a low opinion of me, don't you, Cruz?'

'Look at it from my point of view.' He balled his hands on his hips. 'I come out here to find you giggling like a schoolgirl and one of my best trainers stuffing his wallet back into his pocket. What am I supposed to think?'

Aspen's gaze was icily steady on his. 'That he was showing me pictures of his children being dragged along by the family goat.'

A beat passed in which she wouldn't have been surprised if Cruz had turned and walked away as he had the night before. It seemed to be his *modus operandi* when confronted with anything remotely emotional. Only he didn't.

'I'm sorry,' he said abruptly, raking a hand through his hair. 'I might have overreacted.'

Aspen had never had a man apologise to her before and it completely took the wind out of her sails. 'Well, okay…'

For the first time in her dealings with him he looked a tad uncomfortable. 'I didn't come here to quarrel with you.'

'What *did* you come here for? If you're checking on Bandit's cankers I had a look at the affected hoof before and it's completely healed.'

Cruz frowned. 'That's for the vet to decide, not you.'

'The vet was busy and I know what I'm doing. I'm one semester away from becoming a fully qualified vet. Plus, I've treated a couple of our horses for the disease. So,' she couldn't resist adding, 'not just marrying to secure my future, then.'

A muscle ticked in his jaw. 'You enjoyed telling me that, didn't you?'

'It did feel rather good, yes.'

They stared at each other and then his mouth kicked up at the corners. 'I suppose you want another apology?'

What she wanted was for him to stop smiling and scowl again so she could catch her breath. 'Would it be too much to hope for, do you think?'

'Probably.'

Aspen couldn't hold back a grin and quickly ducked down to pick up Bandit's rear hoof and clean it.

'You've changed,' he said softly.

She looked up and he nodded to the tool in her hand.

'You used to be much more of a princess type.'

'Really?' Her green eyes sparkled with amusement. 'That's how you saw me?'

'That's how all the boys saw you.' He shrugged. 'We got your horse ready and you rode it and then we brushed it down at the end. Back then you wouldn't have even known how to use one of those.'

Aspen grimaced and went back to work on the horse. 'That was because my grandfather wouldn't let me work with the horses. He had very clear ideas on a woman's place in the world. It was why my mother left. She didn't really talk to me about him, but I remember overhearing her talking to a friend and saying that he didn't understand anyone else's opinion but his own.'

Satisfied that the horse's feet were clean, Aspen patted her rump and collected the wooden toolbox. 'You're done for the day, girl.'

She glanced up as Cruz continued to block the doorway. The sound of someone moving tack around further along the stable rattled between them.

'Why did you set me up that night?'

The suddenness of the question and the harshness of his tone jolted her.

'What are you talking about?' She couldn't think how she had set him up, but—

'Eight years ago. You and your *fiancé*.'

'Fiancé?'

She frowned and then realised that he was talking about the night her grandfather had found them. She had no idea what he meant by setting him up, but it shocked her that he thought she'd been engaged to Chad at the time. Then she recalled her grandfather's vitriolic outburst. Something she'd shoved into the deepest recess of her mind.

She grimaced as it all came rushing back. 'Chad and I weren't actually engaged that night,' she said slowly.

'Your grandfather certainly thought you were.'

'That's because I later learned that he had accepted Chad's proposal on my behalf.'

Cruz swore. 'You're saying he forced you to go along with it?'

Aspen hesitated. 'No. I could have turned him down.'

'But you didn't?'

'No, but I certainly didn't consider myself engaged when I walked into the stables and saw you there.'

'How about when you kissed me?'

Aspen shifted uncomfortably. 'No, not then either.'

'That still doesn't answer my question.'

Aspen couldn't remember his question, her mind so full of memories and guilt. 'What question?'

'Why you set me up.'

She shook her head. 'I don't really understand what you mean by that.'

Cruz took in her wary gaze, frustration and desire biting into him like an annoying insect. 'You're saying it was a coincidence that your grandfather just *happened* to come across us and then just *happened* to kick me off the property, thereby paving the way for Anderson to take over as captain of the dream team?'

Her eyes widened with what appeared to be genuine shock. 'I would never…' She blinked as if she was trying to clear her thoughts. 'Grandfather said it was your decision to leave Ocean Haven.'

Cruz scoffed at the absurdity of her statement. 'It was one of those "you can go under your own steam or mine" type of offers,' he said bitterly.

But he could admit to a little resentment, couldn't he? He'd given Charles Carmichael eleven years of abject devotion that had been repaid with anger and accusations and the revocation of every promise the old man had ever made him.

Memories he'd rather obliterate than verbalise turned his tone harsh. 'He accused me of *deflowering* his precious *engaged* granddaughter and you let him believe it.'

'I don't remember that,' she said softly. 'I told him afterwards that we hadn't been together.'

Cruz wasn't interested in another apology. 'So you said.'

'But you still don't believe me?'

'It's irrelevant.'

'I don't think it is. I can hear in your voice that it still pains you and I don't blame you. I should never have let him think what he did. Not even for a second.'

'What you can hear in my voice is not pain but absolute disgust.'

He stepped closer to her, noting how small and fragile she looked, her shoulders narrow, her limbs slender and fine. He knew the taste of her skin, as well as her scent.

'When it happened...' He forced himself to focus. '*Then* I was upset. Devastated, if you want to know the truth. I thought your grandfather and I were equals. I thought he respected me. Maybe even cared for me.' He snorted out a breath and thrust his hand through his hair. 'I thought wrong. Do you know what he told me?'

Cruz had no idea why he was telling her something so deeply private but somehow the words kept coming.

'He told me I wasn't good enough for his granddaughter. He didn't want your lily-white blood mixing with that of a second-class *Mexicano*.'

'But my blood isn't lily-white. My mother saw to that in a fit of rebellion. My grandfather could never get past her decision and because they were both stubborn neither one could offer the other an olive branch. My mother wanted to go home to The Farm *so* many times.'

Aspen swallowed past the lump in her throat.

'But my grandfather had kicked her out. It was the same with you. Two days after you left he had a stroke and I'm sure it was because he had lost you. Of course no one outside the family knew about it, but I knew it had to do with what happened and I felt terrible. Ashamed of myself. But I was scared, Cruz.'

She looked at him with remorseful eyes and no matter what he thought of her it was impossible to doubt her sincerity.

'You know my grandfather's temper. I didn't know what he'd do to me.'

'Nothing,' Cruz bit out. 'He was angry at me, not you. He thought the world of you.'

'As long as I did what he wanted.' She shivered. 'I was so frightened when I arrived at Ocean Haven. I'd heard about the place from my mother and I'd loved it from a small child. I'd never met my grandfather before and I was determined that he wouldn't hate me. And he didn't. But nor did he like me questioning him or going against his wishes. At first that was okay, because I was little, but as I got older it became harder to always be agreeable. That night...' She stopped and looked at him curiously. 'Why didn't you defend yourself against him? Why didn't you tell him that it was *me* who had kissed *you*?'

'It hadn't exactly been one-way.' He ran a hand through his hair. 'And you looked...frightened.'

Aspen gave him a small smile. 'I was that, all right. I'd never seen him in such a rage. I didn't know what to do and I froze. It's a horrible reaction I've never been able to shake when I'm truly petrified. That night, if he had found out that I instigated things with you after he'd told me I was expected to marry Chad, I thought...I thought...'

Cruz briefly closed his eyes. 'You thought he'd disown you like he had your mother.'

The truth of what had happened that night was like a slap in the face.

'It seems silly now, but...'

'It was like history repeating itself. Your mother with the ski instructor...you with the lowly polo player.'

'*I* didn't think that, but he was so angry.' She shuddered at the memory. 'And I never wanted to leave the one place my mother loved so much. She used to talk about it all the time. Do you know that skewed horseshoe wedged between two roof beams in the stable?'

Cruz knew it. Old Charlie had grumbled about it when-ever he was in a bad mood.

'Apparently years ago Mum and Uncle Joe were playing hooky with a bunch of them and when she was losing she got in a terrible snit and aimed one at his head.' Aspen laughed softly, as if she were remembering her mother recounting the story. 'Unfortunately she was a terrible shot and released it too soon. It went shooting up towards the roof and somehow it got stuck. Which was lucky for my uncle because she obviously put her back into it.' She smiled. 'Every time I see it, it's as if she's still here with me.'

She looked at him.

'That night I was so angry with my grandfather for ignoring my wishes that I went to the stable to talk to her. When you showed up and you weren't dressed properly I… I can't explain it rationally.'

Her eyes flitted away and then she seemed to force them back to his.

'I had wanted to kiss you for so long and I wasn't thinking clearly. I know you don't want to hear this but I am sorry, Cruz. I should have stood up for you. But I was selfishly worried about myself and—'

Cruz cupped her face in his hands and kissed her. Lightly. 'It's okay. I remember his temper.'

Aspen gave him a wobbly smile. 'I think I inherited that from him.'

He shook his head, his thumbs stroking her cheekbones. 'You're not scary when you're angry. You're beautiful.'

She made a noise somewhere between a snort and a cough and he couldn't resist kissing her again, his lips lingering and sipping at hers.

This time the noise she made was one of pleasure, and Cruz slid his hand into her hair to hold her head steady, nudging the toolbox out of his way with his knee so that he could shift closer. She pressed into him and he wrapped his other hand around her waist, deepening the kiss. Slowly.

Deliberately drawing out the sweet anticipation of it for both of them.

Aspen's arms rose, linked around his neck and time passed. How much, he couldn't have said.

Slowly she drew back, lifting her long lashes to reveal eyes glazed with passion. 'Wow...' she whispered.

Wow was right.

She moistened her lower lip, her eyes flitting from his, and he frowned. He could have sworn he saw a touch of apprehension in them. He nipped at her lower lip, kissed her again.

With a thousand questions pounding through his head— not least why she seemed nervous when it came to intimacy—he reluctantly ended the searing kiss and leant his forehead against hers. Their breaths mingled, hot and heavy.

'I don't hate you, Aspen,' he said, answering her question of the previous night. Her bewitching green eyes returned to his and he found himself saying, 'I have a formal dinner at the hotel tonight. Come with me.'

Aspen felt dazzled. By the conversation. By his sweet, tender kisses. By the piercing ache in her pelvis that made a mockery of her previous experiences with Chad. 'I'd like that...'

And she did—right up until she found an emerald-green gown laid out on her bed next to black stiletto sandals still inside their box.

Standing stock-still in the centre of the spare room Aspen stared at the exquisite gown.

'Don't wear that. You look awful in it. Here. Put this on.'

Aspen shivered. Chad's voice was so clear in her head he might as well have been standing beside her.

Cruz wasn't Chad. She knew that. But somehow her stomach still felt cramped. Because the dress symbolised some sort of ownership. Some sort of control. And she knew she couldn't give him that—not over her.

It made her realise just what she'd been thinking when he had invited her to the dinner. She'd been thinking it was a date. That it was real.

But this wasn't real. She wouldn't even be here if it wasn't for the deal he had offered her. A deal she had accepted and still hadn't fulfilled. Which she needed to do to keep Ocean Haven. How had she forgotten that? How had she forgotten that he was trying to steal it away from her?

But she knew how. He'd kissed her so tenderly, so reverently, it had been as if eight years had fallen away between them. And she couldn't think like that. Because as much as she hated the coldness of the deal they had struck she also knew that she couldn't afford to feel anything. She couldn't afford to want anything from him other than money. That way was fraught with disaster. It would turn her from an independent woman in charge of her own destiny back into the people-pleaser she had tried to be for her grandfather. For Chad.

She stared at the dress. Cruz was an extraordinarily wealthy man who was used to getting what he wanted. For some reason he had decided that he wanted her. For a night. But that didn't mean she had to wear clothes he'd chosen as well.

Before she could think too much about it she strode out into the living room. The sun was hanging low in the sky and it illuminated his fit body as he stood in front of the window, talking into his cell phone.

As if sensing her presence he turned, scanned her face and the dress she was holding, and told whomever he was talking to that he had to go.

She held the dress out to him. 'I can't wear this.'

He frowned. 'It doesn't fit?'

'No. Yes. Actually, I don't know. I haven't tried it on.'

He smiled. 'Then what's the problem?'

'The problem is—' She dropped her hand and paced away from him. 'The problem is that I'm not a possession you can dress up whenever you like. The problem is I'm an independent woman who has some idea about how to dress herself and doesn't need to be told what to wear by some high-powered male who has to own everything.'

A heavy silence fell over the room as soon as her spiel had finished but somehow her words hung between them like a hideously long banner dragged through the sky by a biplane.

'I take it your grandfather didn't like your choice in outfits?' He dropped into a plush sofa. 'Or was it Anderson?'

For a minute his astute questions floored her. 'Chad has *nothing* to do with this,' she bit out.

His beautiful black eyes glittered with confidence and Aspen was suddenly embarrassed to realise that she had just exposed a part of herself she hadn't intended to.

'At some point we need to talk about him.'

Aspen felt her heart hammer inside her chest. 'We so do not.'

His eyes became hooded. 'We will, but not now. As to the other.' He waved his hand at the emerald silk crushed in her hand. 'It's just a dress, Aspen. I assume you didn't pack anything formal?'

'No.' Deciding to ignore her embarrassment, she forged on. 'But I can buy my own clothes if I need to.'

Clearly exasperated, he looked at her from under long thick lashes. 'Fine. I'll forward you the bill.'

Aspen could tell he had no intention of doing that. 'You may have bought a night with me, Cruz, but that doesn't mean you own me.'

'I don't want to own you.' He laid his arm along the back of the sofa. 'Wear it. Don't wear it. It's irrelevant to me.'

'What *is* relevant to you?' she asked, goaded by his

nonchalant attitude. 'Because it seems to me that you've cut yourself off from everything that could have meaning in your life other than work. Your family. Your polo playing—' Aspen stopped, breathlessly aware that he had risen during her tirade and that he was nowhere near as relaxed as he had appeared.

'The dress was a peace offering.' He grabbed his suit jacket from the back of the nearby chair. 'But you can bin it for all I care.'

Feeling all at sea as he stalked out of the penthouse, Aspen returned to her room and leant against the closed door.

A peace offering?

She felt stupid and knew that she had acted like a drama queen. And she knew why. She was tense. The thought of sex with Cruz was hanging over her head like a stalactite. And felt just as deadly.

Glancing at the bed, she ignored the tight feeling in her chest and tossed the dress onto it. Then she stripped off and scalded herself with a hot shower, all the while knowing that as she plucked and preened and soaped herself with the delicious vanilla-scented soap that she was doing so with Cruz in mind. Which made her feel worse. This wasn't a romance. It was a deal.

A deal that would end as soon as they'd slept together.

A deal that could still go wrong if her uncle decided that he needed the money Cruz was willing to part with to turn Ocean Haven into a horrible hotel.

Trying not to dwell on that, she rolled her eyes at herself when she realised she'd changed her hairstyle five times. She looked at the spiralling mess. All her fiddling had turned her hair to frizz. *Great.*

Salvaging it as best she could, she stomped back into the bedroom and spied the offending gown she had flung onto the bed. Even skewed it rippled, and dared any woman not to want to wear it.

And given the contents of her suitcase what choice did she really have? None. And she hated that because she'd had so little choice in what had happened to her growing up on Ocean Haven. After Chad she had vowed she'd never be beholden to anyone again—especially not a man. But one night with Cruz didn't make her beholden to him, did it?

Once he'd lent her the money and she'd paid him back, as she would the other investors, they would be back on an equal footing. She exhaled. One night, straight up, and then she was home free.

Why did that leave her feeling so empty?

She looked again at the dress. Grimaced. Trust him to have such superb taste.

CHAPTER EIGHT

'ARE YOU EVEN listening to what I'm saying?'

Cruz glanced at Ricardo, who was debriefing him on who was attending the formal dinner that night and how impressed the Chinese delegation were with the facilities. The Sunset Bar, where they had decided to catch up for a drink before the evening proceedings, was full to bursting with excited players and polo experts from all over the globe.

'Of course,' he lied. 'Go on.'

Ricardo frowned, but thankfully continued working his way through the list.

Cruz studied it also, but his mind was elsewhere. More specifically his mind was weighing up how he was going to steal The Farm out from under Aspen's gorgeous fingertips when he now knew the truth about that fateful night.

He took a healthy swig of his tequila. He'd been *so* sure she had done him wrong eight years ago he'd been blind to any other possibility. *Tainted*, he realised belatedly. Tainted by his own deep-seated feelings of inferiority and hurt pride.

Hell.

He couldn't escape the knowledge that seeing Aspen again had unearthed a wealth of bitterness he hadn't even realised he'd buried deep inside himself—resentments he'd let fester but that no longer seemed relevant.

What is *relevant to you?*

Hell, that woman had a way of working her way inside his head. But as much as he hated that he knew in good conscience he couldn't take Ocean Haven away from her. He'd never be able to face himself in the mirror again if he did. But what to do? Because if he also let her continue with her foolhardy plan to borrow thirty million dollars to keep it she'd be bankrupt within a year.

Of course that wasn't his problem. She was an adult and could take care of herself. But some of that old protectiveness he had always felt towards her was seeping back in and refused to go away. He wanted to fix everything for her, but she was so fiercely guarded, so intent on doing everything herself. It was madness. But so was the fact that he couldn't stop thinking about her. That he even *wanted* to fix things for her in the first place.

Realising that Ricardo was waiting for him to say something, Cruz nodded thoughtfully. 'Sam Harris is playing tomorrow. Got it.'

'Actually,' Ricardo said patiently, 'Sam Harris is sick. Tommy Hassenberger is taking his place.'

'Send Sam a bottle of tequila.'

'I already sent flowers.'

Cruz shook his head at his brother. 'And you think you need a *wife*?'

Normally his brother would have returned his light ribbing, but to Cruz's chagrin he didn't this time.

'What's up?' he said instead.

Cruz rubbed his jaw and realised he should have shaved again. 'Nothing.'

'You're a million miles away. It wouldn't have anything to do with Aspen Carmichael, would it?'

Bingo.

'If I say no, you'll assume I'm lying, and if I say yes, you'll want to know why.'

Ricardo shook his head and laughed. '*Dios mio*, you've got it bad.'

Cruz dismissed Ricardo's comment. He *wanted* her badly, yes, and he was happy to admit that, but he didn't *have* it bad in the way his brother was implying.

A hush fell over the bar at the same time as the skin on the back of his neck started to prickle. Then Ricardo let out a low whistle under his breath.

'*Mi, oh, mi....*'

Slowly Cruz turned his head to find Aspen framed in the open double glass doorway of the bar like something out of a 1950s Hollywood extravaganza, the silky green gown he'd bought her flowing around her slender figure like coloured water. His mouth went dry. The halterneck dress was deceptively simple at the front but so beautifully crafted it lovingly moulded to her shape exactly as it was supposed to. She'd pinned her hair up in a soft, timeless bun—which must mean she had a fair amount of skin showing, as he was pretty sure the dress dipped quite low at the back.

Okay, make that completely backless, he corrected, fighting a primitive urge to bundle her up in his arms and return her to his room. His bed.

She hadn't spotted him yet, and when a male voice called out her name Cruz watched her turn her head, the wispy tendrils of hair she had left to frame her face dancing golden beneath the halogen lighting. Her expression softened as she spied a few of his polo players lounging in the club chairs that circled a small wooden table.

She walked towards them and Cruz tried not to react, but it was impossible to stop his gut from tightening as the men watched her with unrestrained lust in their eyes.

She looked so delicate.

So sensual.

So *his*.

The need to stamp his ownership all over her took hold and he didn't bother to contain it. For right now, for tonight, she was his—and he didn't care who knew it. In fact, the more who did the better. It would save him from having to keep tabs on her during dinner, and the four European jocks already halfway to being tanked would, he knew, be the best candidates to spread the news.

As conversation once again resumed in the bar he ignored Ricardo's keen gaze and went to her.

She had her back to him and he felt her jump as his thigh lightly grazed her hip. She looked up and he bent his head, let his eyes linger on her mouth, gratified by her quick intake of breath.

If it were possible, the more time he spent with her the more time he *wanted* to spend with her. It was a sobering thought, if he'd been in the mood to care.

He cupped Aspen's elbow in his palm. 'Gentlemen, if you'll excuse us?'

Slowly each man registered Cruz's proprietorial manner, but only Tommy Hassenberger had the nerve to look disgruntled. 'Looks like I'm too late,' he complained.

'You were too late when you were born, Tommy,' one of his friends joked, making the others laugh.

Aspen grinned, said she'd catch up with them at the formal dinner, and then felt intoxicated as Cruz placed his hand on the small of her back to guide her from the room, the heat of his palm scorching her bare skin.

She hadn't known what to expect when she had entered the bar but she had decided to try and relax. To try and forget about their deal and her fears and just brave it out. Cruz had invited her to dinner—a formal event, not a date—and for all she knew that was a peace offering as well.

'You wore the dress,' he said, his gravelly voice stroking her already heightened senses.

'Yes. I couldn't not in the end. Thank you.'

'You look stunning in it.'

The look he gave her made her burn.

Aspen took in his superbly cut tuxedo. 'You look—' *Simply divine.* 'Nice too,' she croaked.

He gave her a small smile. 'Aspen, I need to tell you something.'

Cruz gazed down at the utterly stunning woman at his side and a ball of emotion rushed through him. Seeing her like this…having her beside him…all the animosity of the past fell away and he just wanted to take her upstairs and make love to her with a need that floored him.

'What is it?'

Aspen tilted her head and Cruz heard a roaring in his ears as their eyes connected. Reality seemed suspended and—

'Señor Rodriguez, sir, the first lot of guests are assembled in the Rosa Room.'

Cruz turned towards his head waiter. 'Thank you, Paco. I'll be along in a minute.'

'Certainly.'

The waiter inclined his head and left and Cruz lifted Aspen's fingers to his lips. He could see her pulse racing and his did the same.

'I wish I'd never planned this idiotic dinner.'

'It's not idiotic.' She smiled up at him, her eyes almost on a level with his chin because she was wearing the stilettos. 'It's to welcome honoured guests to your flagship hotel for tomorrow's tournament. It's important.'

Not half as important as what he wanted to be doing with her upstairs right now.

His nostrils flared as he fought to control the urge to drag her into the nearest darkened corner. On one level he thought he should be concerned about the intensity of his hunger for her, but on another he just couldn't bring himself to examine it. There was something about her that sent his baser instincts off the scale.

Nothing a night of straightforward, short-term hot sex wouldn't cure.

He smiled at the thought and, with the situation once again under his control, he tucked her elegant hand in the crook of his elbow and prayed for the evening formalities to fly by.

The dinner took all night. As it was supposed to.

The first course had been Mushroom-something. Aspen couldn't remember and Cruz, possibly noticing her picking at it dubiously, had swapped it for his goat's cheese soufflé. Then there'd been the main course. Beef or chicken. This time Aspen had swapped with him when she'd seen him eyeing her steak.

He'd smiled, grazed her chin with his knuckles and then resumed talking to two well-dressed Asian men, who'd nodded with polite restraint. Now and then he'd twined his fingers with hers when she'd left her hand on the tabletop while he talked, as if it was the most natural thing in the world for him to do. As if this really was a date.

Aspen had chatted to the wife of the Mayor, who was very down to earth and full of Latin passion, and their daughter who was studying to be a doctor. They'd swapped war stories of bad essay topics, boring lecturers and horror exams and then it had been time for dessert.

She was full. Even though she'd hardly eaten a thing.

Her dinner companions excused themselves, and Aspen was just contemplating whether she should move to the other side of the table to speak with an older woman who sat on her own when Cruz slid his fingers through hers again. His hand was so much bigger than hers, his skin tone darker, the hairs on the back of his wrists absurdly attractive.

He stroked his thumb over her palm and goosebumps raced themselves up her arm.

He glanced in her direction, brought her hand briefly to his lips and then answered one of the Asian men's questions.

The Mayor's daughter returned and Cruz dropped Aspen's hand as the girl produced a photo of her horse on her phone. Aspen made polite responses, all the time disturbingly aware of the man beside her.

Something had changed between them since she'd come downstairs. He was behaving as she imagined a man in love would behave. Little intimate glances, tucking her hair behind her ear, pouring her water, holding her hand...

Chad had seemed nice in the beginning too. Wooing her. Treating her lovingly. Somehow it had all come unstuck the year Cruz had left and her grandfather had been too sick to send the team to England. Chad had been unable to get a permanent ride that year and had started drinking more. By the time their wedding had rolled around she'd barely recognised him as the man who had courted her and treated her so deferentially. He'd moved back home when his father had threatened to halve his trust fund, and his father had used the opportunity to encourage Chad to get a real job. Aspen had tried to smooth things over but that had only seemed to make him resentful.

On their wedding night— No, she didn't want to remember that.

She glanced at Cruz to find him deep in conversation. Would he be rough? She swallowed, her gaze drawn to his hands, wrapped around a wine glass. He stroked the slender stem with the pad of his thumb. Aspen recalled how he had stroked her lips the same way and heat erupted low in her belly. For a man with such size and strength he had been gentle. Suddenly his thumb stopped moving and Aspen felt the air between them shift even before her eyes connected with his.

Her mouth dried and her heart thumped. Fear and desire commingled until she felt emotionally wrung out.

'Aspen?'

She glanced up but didn't really see him.

'Everything okay?'

Oh, God, that deep, sensual voice so close to her ear. She couldn't help it. She trembled. Then pulled herself together.

'Fine.' *Just me being a nincompoop.*

Nincompoop? Her mother had used that word when she'd been laughing at herself.

A wave of sadness overtook her and immediately made her think of Ocean Haven. Her horses. Her mother. Aspen had gained wealth by moving in with her grandfather but not love, and certainly not security.

Cruz moved his hand to the back of her chair. 'You look miles away.'

A wave of panic washed through her and she made the mistake of glancing up at him.

As soon as their eyes met his sharpened with concern. 'Hey, what's wrong?'

'Nothing.' She forced a smile. 'I just need to go to the bathroom.'

He scanned her face but thankfully didn't push her. 'Don't be long. We'll go when you get back.'

Oh, help.

She got up, stumbled and snagged the tablecloth with her leg. Cruz leaned over and held it while she straightened up. The deliciously sexy gown he had bought her swayed around her body and settled. She felt his eyes on her as she started to walk away, the dress floating around her legs as light as butterfly wings. Of course that was nothing compared to the butterflies using her belly as a trampoline.

Once in the bathroom she told herself to calm down and splashed cold water on her wrists, dabbed it on her cheeks. She checked her make-up, shocked to see her face so flushed. It was because every time he touched her she thought of sex.

A woman smiled at her in the mirror and Aspen dropped her gaze lest the woman accurately read her mind. Then she realised how rude that was and raised her eyes only to find the person had gone.

She let out a shaky laugh at her absurd behaviour. She felt like… She felt like… She frowned. She couldn't remember ever feeling this nervous.

Well, maybe she could. On her wedding day. She'd had a similar fluttering feeling in her stomach then that had turned out to be a bad omen.

She stared at herself. Fear knotted her insides. She couldn't do this. Her eyes looked like two huge dots in her face. She just couldn't do it. She was so anxious she'd probably throw up all over him.

An older woman entered the bathroom and Aspen pretended to be wiping her hands.

She'd have to tell Cruz.

Would it mean she'd still get the money if she backed out?

Oh, who cares about the money? This was no longer about the money. This was now about self-preservation. This was about going back to the wonderful, predictable life that she loved.

Yes, but there won't be that life if you don't go through with this.

She'd backed herself into a corner and the only way out was through Cruz. A man who, for all his surface arrogance, genuinely cared about his family and was smart. And also ruthless. He would chew her up and spit her out without a backward glance if she let him.

'Let's not forget why you're here, Aspen,' she told her reflection softly.

He was pitting himself against her for Ocean Haven. Her farm. She should hate him for that alone but she didn't, she realised. She didn't hate him at all. Because she had come to understand him a little better. Understand what he had thought of her. What had shaped him as a boy. What had shaped him as a man.

How did you hate someone you instinctively sensed was good underneath? And what did that even matter?

Shaking her head at her reflection, she refastened a few loosened strands of hair and wondered where all her positive self-talk had run off to.

Maybe down the toilet.

She smiled at her lame attempt at humour and nearly walked straight into Cruz where he leant against the wall opposite the ladies' room.

'You were taking so long I got worried. I was just about to go in but I didn't want to surprise you.'

'I would have been okay.' She let out a shaky breath. 'It's the old lady in the cubicle you might have had some trouble with.'

Cruz laughed and it broke the tension. He held out his hand. 'Shall we go?'

She looked at his perfect, handsome face. Then his hand, palm up. He was strong, maybe stronger than Chad, but he wasn't nasty. Even when he'd thought she had done him wrong he still hadn't picked on her the way Chad would have done. No, Cruz was arrogant and controlling, but he was honest and straight down the line. A straight arrow. Black and white. No shades of grey.

'Aspen?'

She saw hunger and desire in his eyes and it made her feel hot all over. Maybe she could do this. *Maybe.*

She glanced at his hand, wondered if she was as crazy as her uncle had suggested and placed hers in it.

He smiled.

She swallowed.

It wasn't until they were halfway across the foyer that she saw a familiar figure—a man—leaning against the reception desk. He had his back to her, so she couldn't see his face, but he was average height with blond hair and a slightly stocky bodybuilder's physique.

Chad?

Cruz pressed the lift button and Aspen's attention was momentarily snagged by their reflection in the gold-finished doors. They looked good together, she thought. He was tall and broad, and she looked feminine and almost otherworldly in the beautiful green dress.

His eyes met hers and she couldn't look away.

Then the lift doors opened. Aspen snuck another quick glance over her shoulder but the man she had spotted wasn't there. She let out a relieved breath. After their last acrimonious argument Chad had kept to his own part of the world and she to hers.

Still, she stabbed repeatedly at the penthouse button and only realised how questionable her behaviour looked when she noticed Cruz's bemused expression and realised he hadn't swiped his security tag across the electronic panel.

His eyebrows rose and Aspen's gaze dropped to the space between their feet, her heart beating too fast. Seeing the man who might or might not have been her ex-husband had been terrible timing. Just when she'd begun to think maybe her night with Cruz would be all right it was as if the powers that be had sent her a message to take care.

To remind her that being in a man's control was when a woman was at her most vulnerable.

As the lift ascended Cruz pushed away from the mirror-panelled wall and invaded her space, startling her out of her dark reverie when he placed his warm hands either side of her waist.

'Okay, talk to me. You're as nervous as a pony facing the bridle for the first time. The same as you were last night.'

Aspen gave a low laugh at his analogy and jumped when his thumbs stroked her hip bones through the dress. She couldn't tell him she thought she'd just seen Chad. That would raise a whole host of questions that she did not want to answer. And what if she was wrong? Then she'd just look stupid. Or paranoid.

'I'm fine.'

'You're shaking.'

Was she?

He gave her a look. 'Is it the deal? Because—'

'It's not the deal. Actually I'd forgotten all about that again.'

Her answer seemed to please him but she didn't have time to consider his satisfied—'Good.'—because the lift doors opened.

When he'd released her he placed his hand on the small of her back as he ushered her through to the living room. The housekeeper had been and the room was cast with shadows by the floor lamps that had been switched on for their convenience.

'Do you want a drink?'

'Yes, please.'

She'd said that too loudly and his eyes narrowed.

'Of…?'

Aspen forced a smile. 'Gin and tonic.' She winced. She hated gin and tonic.

She wandered over to the wall to study one of the paintings she'd admired the evening before but never taken the time to look at. An overhead light outlined it perfectly and she gasped.

'That's a Renoir.'

'I know.'

He was right behind her and she heard the tinkle of ice as he handed her the drink she didn't want.

'You're not having one?'

'No.' He perched on the arm of a nearby sofa, watching her. 'Something wrong with it?'

'What?'

He motioned patiently towards the highball in her hand. 'Your drink?'

'No. It's fine. At least, I'm sure it's fine.' It was all about maintaining control. If she did that she could get through this. 'Look, maybe we should just…start.'

'Start?'

Aspen could have kicked herself, and she moved towards a side table so she could let out a discreet breath and put the drink down. She knew he hadn't taken his eyes off her and she told herself that he wanted her. She'd felt how aroused he had been last night, and again in the stable that day. He had felt huge!

So why had he stopped? Was he struggling to maintain an erection with her as Chad had done? She shuddered. On those occasions Chad had been particularly vile.

Cruz tilted his head and looked as if he was about to say something, and then he changed his mind. Instead he uncurled his large frame and came towards her until he practically loomed over her. Then he reached for her hair.

She didn't mean to do it, of course, but she flinched and his hand stilled. 'I'm just going to take your hair down.'

She stared at his chest and tried to slow her heartbeat.

'Is that okay?'

She nodded, not trusting herself to speak.

'Turn around.'

It took all of her willpower to give him that modicum of control, but when she did turn around he stroked her shoulders.

'You have a beautiful back. Lean and supple. Strong.'

He kneaded the bunched muscles either side of her neck and her involuntary sigh of pleasure filled the quiet room.

'That feels so good. I know I must be really tight.'

Cruz groaned inwardly, knowing she hadn't meant that comment the way his depraved mind had interpreted it. Yes, she did feel tight. Too tight. Too nervous.

He wanted to ask her what was wrong, but she moaned softly and her head lolled on the graceful stem of her neck and the question died in his throat.

All through dinner he'd imagined doing this. Touching her, tasting her. He'd been harder than stone all night and he wasn't sure if he'd committed to five hotels in China or fifty. Nor did he care. Right now he'd put a hundred on Mars if someone asked him to.

Aspen moaned again and shifted beneath his pressing thumbs.

'Harder or softer?' he asked, the rough timbre of his voice reflecting his deep arousal.

He heard her breath catch, and then his did as well as her gorgeous bottom brushed his fly.

'Harder,' she whispered, and a shudder ripped through him.

The musky perfume of her skin was ambrosia to his senses and he trailed soft kisses across her shoulders. Her head fell forward and she braced her hands on the side table in front of her. Cruz registered her position on a purely primal level and knew all he'd have to do was lift that long silk skirt, tear whatever excuse for a pair of panties she was hiding underneath, bend her a little more forward and slide right into her—and he very nearly did.

But he wanted more of her taste in his mouth first, and with unsteady hands he gripped the side of her waist and trailed tiny moist kisses down the column of her spine until he reached the small of her back.

She undulated for him, arching backwards, and unable to hold himself back any longer he rose, spun her around to face him and slanted his mouth across hers. Not softly, as he had done earlier in the stables—he was too far gone for that—but hard, with barely leashed power and a deep driving hunger to be inside her.

She opened for him instantly, her fingers impatient as they delved into his hair to anchor him to her. That was okay with him. He barely noticed the bite of her short nails, concentrating instead on the throbbing sense of satisfaction as his tongue filled her mouth. He tasted coffee and cream and couldn't suppress a groan.

Somehow some of her earlier hesitation seeped into the minute part of his brain that still functioned on an intellectual level and he attempted to steady himself—before he just dragged her to the floor and had done with it.

Then her tongue stroked his and his mind gave out. Sensation hot and strong coursed through him, just as it had every other time he'd kissed her, and he couldn't help curving her closer so that they touched everywhere.

The silky fabric of her dress slid against his jacket in an erotic parody of skin on skin. Which was what he wanted. What he needed. And, keeping his mouth firmly on hers, he shucked out of it and then lashed at the buttons on his shirt.

She moaned, her warm hands pushing the fabric off his body as she shaped his arms and his shoulders before clinging once more around his neck.

Cruz reached behind her neck. His fingers felt clumsy in his desperation as he finally managed to undo the two pearl-like buttons that held the top of the dress together.

Aroused to an unbearable pitch, he smoothed a hand down to the small of her back, his lips cruising along her jawline until he could tug on the lobe of her ear. She was wearing tiny gold studs and he tongued one as he bit down gently on her flesh and brought his hands around to cradle both breasts in the palms of his hands. She trembled delightfully and her responsiveness rocked him to his core.

His thumb caught her nipple and she cried out, gripping him tighter. Cruz knew that neither of them was going to make it to the bedroom so he didn't even try. Instead he lifted her onto the side table and hoped it would hold.

It did, and he pulled back and looked down at her.

Her nipples pebbled enticingly beneath his lingering gaze and he plumped one breast up. 'You're so beautiful,' he breathed, taking the rosy tip into his mouth.

Arousal beat through his body, hot and insistent, and he urged her thighs wider so that he could settle his erection between her legs. Unfortunately the table wasn't high enough for him to take her on it and he knew he'd have to lift her onto him when the time came.

'Thank heavens you're wearing a dress,' he growled around her tight, wet nipple, his impatient hands delving beneath the reams of fabric to find her.

Moments later he felt her panic in the stiffening of her thighs and the press of her fingernails on his shoulders.

'Wait!'

His blurred mind tried to take in the change and he mentally pulled back.

'We might need some lubricant,' she blurted out against his neck.

Lubricant?

Cruz stilled, and was struck by how slight and vulnerable her body felt compared to his much larger frame curved over her. Instantly his libido cooled as he recalled those times she had flinched away from him when he'd reached for her. He frowned. Had she *never* experienced pleasure during sex?

He brought one hand up between them to cup her jaw and brought her eyes to his. 'Aspen, what's wrong?'

'I'm just…' She licked her lips, her mortified gaze flitting sideways. 'I don't have much natural lubrication. I should have told you earlier.'

Stunned, Cruz could only stare at her. He could tell she was serious but he had briefly felt her moist heat through her panties and knew she needed extra lubrication the way Ireland needed rain.

As if taking his prolonged silence as a rejection, she shoved his chest hard enough to dislodge him and desperately scooted off the table.

Only her stilettos must have come off when he'd lifted her because her feet tangled in the fabric of her dress and she pitched forward.

Cursing, Cruz grabbed hold of her before she fell. 'Aspen, wait.'

'No. Let me go.'

Ignoring her attempts to break free, he gently tugged her back into his embrace. She immediately buried her head against his neck and he brought one hand up to stroke her hair. His heart thundered in his chest as his dazed mind tried to process what was happening.

He waited until he felt her breathing start to even out and then he leaned back so he could look at her face.

'Who told you that you didn't have any natural lubrication?'

She groaned and burrowed even more fully against him.

Cruz cupped her nape soothingly. 'I know you're embarrassed. Was it Anderson?'

'It happens to some women.'

Cruz had no doubt she was correct, but he had already felt how damp she was through her lace panties and, whatever problems she had, he very much doubted this was one of them.

'I'm sure it does *chiquita*, but it hasn't happened to you.'

She pulled back. 'You're wrong. Chad and I... Can we not talk about this?'

He was going to kill the moron.

Cruz nudged her chin up until her baleful glare met his. He nearly smiled at her thorny gaze but this was too serious. 'Did he hurt you?'

She wet her lips, dropped her eyes.

'Aspen?'

'Oh, all right.' She sighed. 'On our wedding night Chad was... I was anxious. Chad had been drinking heavily and I knew I had made a mistake. Actually, I knew I'd made a mistake even before the wedding, but it became bigger than I was and I didn't know how to stop it. And Chad could be charming.' She gave an empty laugh. 'You might not know that, being a man, but my friends thought he was wonderful. But the alcohol changed him and that night...' She swallowed. 'That night...'

'He raped you,' he said flatly.

'No. It was my fault. I was nervous.'

Cruz barely held himself in check. 'Do *not* blame yourself.' He guided her eyes back up to look at him. 'He would have known that you were nervous.' He cursed under his breath. 'Hell, Aspen. You were all of eighteen.'

She gave him a wobbly smile and Cruz enfolded her in his arms. He held her until he felt her trembling subside.

'He didn't mean to, Cruz. It just wasn't easy.'

Uh-huh. When he did kill him he'd do it slowly.

'It's fine. I knew this would happen anyway. You can let me go.'

Let her go?

She tried to pull away, and when he looked at her she had that same resigned look on her face that she'd had the previous night.

'When I first arrived at Ocean Haven to work for your grandfather,' he began tentatively, 'I missed my family so much I cried myself to sleep every night for a month and I felt pathetic. You were right yesterday when you said it was a lot for a kid to take on. At the time, though, I thought I just needed to man up.'

'Oh, Cruz.'

Her hand curled around his forearm, and even though he knew he was sharing the memory with her to take her mind off her own past part of him still soaked up the comfort of her touch.

'I thought my mother was turning her back on me. That I was an embarrassment to the family.'

'No.' Aspen shook her head fiercely. 'I only met her yesterday but I *know* that can't be true.'

'Probably not. And what Anderson told you isn't true either.' When her eyes fell to the side Cruz tipped her chin up. 'Aspen, you're a beautiful, sensual woman and I want to prove that to you if you'll let me.'

She frowned. 'I don't see how.'

He cupped her face in his hands, halting her words. 'I want you, Aspen. I want to kiss you and touch you and make love to you until all you can think about is how good you feel. The question is, do *you* want that to happen?'

The question might also be what the hell was he talking about? It was one thing to make a woman feel good in bed. It was quite another to want to slay her demons for her.

Ignoring the fact that he had never donned the white knight suit before, and what that meant, Cruz waited for her answer.

And waited.

Finally, still clutching her dress to her chest, her eyes wide and luminous in the over-bright room, she nodded. 'I think so.'

'Then relax and let me take care of you. And, Aspen...?' He waited for her to look at him from beneath the fringe of her dark lashes. 'If you want me to stop at any time, then we'll stop. Understand?'

She paused and her green eyes opened a little wider. 'You'd really do that, wouldn't you?'

For a brief moment Cruz savoured all the ways he would break every bone in Chad Anderson's body, starting with his pompous head and working his way down.

'In a heartbeat, *mi chiquita*. No questions asked.'

CHAPTER NINE

ASPEN BREATHED IN Cruz's warm, musky scent as he carried her to his bedroom and told herself to relax. But it was impossible. She was too embarrassed. Her old panic had returned full force when she'd felt Cruz's warm hand slide between her thighs and now she clung to his neck like a spider monkey as he laid her on the bed.

'Aspen?'

The bedcover was cool at her back and his naked chest was hot at her front as he tried to prise her hands from around his neck. In her earlier fantasies about sex it was romantic and sensual. Dreamy and wonderful. Hot and desperate. This felt awkward and tense.

She didn't look at him as he turned onto his side, visualising how gauche she must appear, with her hair spread out around her and her body partially exposed, with the bodice of her dress undone and metres of silk twisted up around her waist. Keeping her eyes scrunched tight, she adjusted the skirt down her legs.

'Can you turn out the light?' She could feel it burning holes in her retinas even though her eyes were clamped shut.

'I will if it makes you more comfortable, but I won't be able to see you if I do that.'

'That would be the general idea.'

'Open your eyes, *gatita*.'

'Is it a prerequisite?'

His low chuckle had her squinting up at him. He looked lazy and indolent with his head propped in his hands, his gaze extremely male and hot as it met hers. Well, clearly only one of them was feeling awkward and tense.

'You're very comfortable with this, aren't you?'

'You will be too, very soon,' he promised. 'More than comfortable.'

He brought his hand up to her face and started drawing lazy patterns with his finger over her cheeks and nose and down the side of her neck to her collarbone. It wasn't easy for her to give him control, but Aspen lay as still as a stone, slowly recognising that her skin was tingling with a pleasant sensation and that goosebumps had risen up along her upper arms.

'How much pleasure have you actually had during sex, *mi chiquita*?'

She swallowed and would have turned from him then, but his magical finger edged along the loose side of her dress and feathered across her nipple. She sucked in a shallow breath, letting it out on a rush. 'Not much,' she answered honestly. *None* seemed too big an admission to make.

'Mmm...' Cruz ducked his head to her shoulder and trailed a line of kisses to the sensitive curve of her neck. 'Then we'll have to change all that. I am now taking it as my personal mission to teach you about pleasure.'

He shifted closer so that she could feel the heat of his body burn into the side of hers.

'Nothing but pleasure.'

He looked at her as if he wanted to devour her. As if he couldn't think of anything else but her. The thought frightened her, because her desire for him had grown exponentially over the course of a couple of days and she didn't know how that had happened.

He had invaded her thoughts and her dreams and seemed to make a mockery of her declaration that she would never again be at any man's mercy. Because here she was, lying nearly naked on his bed and feeling way out of her depth. And yet as scary as that thought was, as she looked at him like this, his face half in shadow from the bedside lamp, he looked amazing. His strong features and wide shoulders promised to fulfil all of her hidden desires and she felt utterly and completely safe with him, she realised with astonishment. Something she would have said she would never feel again in a man's arms.

Warmth returned deep inside her. Warmth and a sense of wonder that made her feel hot and restless. Her gaze fell to where her hands rested on his gorgeous chest and then she slowly returned her eyes to his. The look in his was both tender and hungry and it made her insides melt.

Reaching up, she stroked the sexy stubble already lining his jaw. 'Make love to me, Cruz. Please.'

As if he'd been waiting for her to say those exact words he took one of her hands and brought her palm to his lips. His answer, 'It will be my pleasure…' rumbled through his chest and arrowed straight into her heart.

His next kiss was hot and deep and sensation swamped her, sending sparks of excitement everywhere, cutting off her ability to think. Her inhibitions and worries seemed to be caught up with some primal desire and this time desire won out.

There was just no room to consider anything other than Cruz's big hands on her body, stroking her, adoring her. His whispered words of encouragement as he discarded her dress and moved her tiny thong down her thighs raised her level of anticipation to an unbearable pitch.

Within seconds she was naked beneath him and his mouth was tracking a path to her breast. Aspen held still, already anticipating the heady pleasure his mouth would bring. And she wasn't disappointed. Cruz drew the tight bud gently into his mouth, licked, circled, nipped and did things to her nipple that were surely illegal. Aspen felt dizzy and her hazy mind didn't even register when his hand slid over the outside of her thighs. Then every neuron in her brain tightened and focused as she felt his hand drift inwards.

'Still with me, *chiquita*?' he asked, blowing warm air across her moist breast.

'Yes, oh, yes.' She curled her hands around the defined muscles in his shoulders. 'But you're still partially dressed.'

'Not for long,' he assured her. 'But let's take care of something first.' He gently pressed her upper body back down on the bed. 'Lie back, *gatita*. This is all for you.'

Aspen complied, but she still tensed when his hand returned to her closed thighs. She half expected him to open them and maybe move over the top of her, to push himself inside her. What she didn't expect was that he would bend one of her knees up and start stroking her leg as one might a domestic cat. Or a startled horse.

And then she couldn't think at all, because he brought his mouth back to her breast and laved the tip with his tongue. She pressed closer, husky little sounds urging him on, and her lower body clenched unbearably with every tug of his lips on her nipple. Then his hand started circling higher on her leg. Slowly. So slowly it was sheer torture. She couldn't stop herself from restlessly trying to turn towards him. She needed weight, she realised, and pressure.

'Patience, *chiquita*,' he implored, his breathing heavy.

'I don't have any,' she groaned, and then gasped as his fingers lightly grazed over the curls between her legs before circling her belly and dipping down again, this time lingering a little longer and pressing a little lower.

Unbelievably Aspen shifted her legs a little wider of her

own accord and knew in that moment that she truly wanted this to happen. That she wanted more. That she wanted all of him. Inside her. Her fear of disappointing him, of failing, of him hurting her was completely eradicated as need spiralled through her and drove everything else out of her mind. If it didn't work out she no longer cared. She just needed *something*. Him!

She waited breathlessly as his finger ran along the seam between her legs again, only to exhale as it continued moving up to link with one of hers.

'Cruz, please...' She curled her free hand around his neck and dragged his mouth back to hers.

'You want me to touch you, *chiquita*?' he said against her lips.

'You know I do.' Then she had a horrid thought. 'Don't you want to?'

He stilled and held her gaze as he brought the hand he held down to the front of his pants. He was huge. That was Aspen's first thought. And her second was that she wanted to see him, touch him.

'Never doubt it,' he said fiercely. 'Never.'

His kiss was hard and hungry and then he wrenched his mouth from hers.

'But I'm trying to go slow. Make sure you're totally ready for me.' He took her hand in his again, linking his fingers over the back of hers. 'And I have something to show you.'

He laid her hand palm-down on her belly and then slowly guided her hand over her silky curls.

'Open your legs wider, *chiquita*,' he murmured beside her ear. 'No. More. Yes, like that...'

And then he directed her hand even lower until, with a gasp, Aspen felt herself as she never had before.

'Oh, my God—that feels...'

'Wet?'

Cruz ran the tip of his tongue around the whorl of her ear and she nearly came off the bed.

He pressed her hand downwards. 'Silky? Sexy?'

Yes!

Lost in a maelstrom of sensation, Aspen closed her eyes and let her feelings take over. She didn't know what to focus on as her fingers slipped over her body, making her want to press upwards.

'And now...' Cruz shifted until he lay on his stomach between her splayed legs, his olive skin dark against the cream bedcovers. 'Now I'm going to taste you.'

Aspen tried to close her legs in a hurry. 'Cruz, you can't.'

He looked up, the skin on his face tight as he held his hands still on her open thighs.

'Let me, Aspen. Remember? I promised you nothing but pleasure.'

Tensing just a little, she let him move her legs wider again and closed her eyes as he dipped down and opened her with his skilled tongue.

She'd heard of men doing this, of course. She had been to an all-girls school, and she knew that some girls liked it and some didn't. She had always put herself in the latter camp. Cruz's low groans of pleasure as he licked and lapped at her sensitive flesh shifted her firmly to the former.

She thought maybe he asked if she was okay, but by that stage he had brought his fingers into play and Aspen couldn't breathe, let alone answer. Her whole body was burning and intensely focused on something that seemed just out of reach. She writhed and twisted beneath him, delighting in the scrape of his stubble against her tender skin, not even registering that she was calling his name until he moved over her.

'It's okay, *chiquita*. Let go.'

Let go? Of what?

And then it happened. Somehow the gentle stroking of his fingers sped up and they moved in such a way that she felt something inside her shift. Within seconds her body had exploded into a thousand tiny pieces.

Distantly she was aware that he had moved down her body again, but she was in such a blissful state of completion she felt as if she was floating.

'Aspen, open your eyes.'

Were her eyes closed again?

Opening them, she saw Cruz watching her.

'How was that?'

She smiled. 'That was the most exquisitely pleasurable experience of my whole life.'

'And I'm just getting started,' he drawled arrogantly.

Aspen laughed, and then her breath caught as he rose over her with latent male grace; his powerful biceps bunched as he completely covered her and took her mouth with his again.

She felt the heavy weight of his erection against her stomach and unbelievably her lower body clenched, needing pressure again. She squirmed upwards, opening her legs automatically.

Groaning, Cruz rolled off her, yanked his pants off in a rustle of fabric and reached into the side drawer for a condom. She watched, completely motionless, as he tore the wrapper apart with his teeth and then held his hard length with one hand while he applied it.

'You keep looking at me like that, *mi gatita*, and I'll have no need for protection,' he husked, his gravelly voice rolling straight to her pelvis.

Aspen felt herself blush, but she didn't look away. He was too mesmerising. Too…

'Beautiful,' she said. 'You're beautiful.'

She ran her hand over his tanned back, briefly marvelling at the smooth heated texture of his skin and the way he trembled beneath her touch. Had *she* done that? Her eyes flew to his and she noticed the sheen of perspiration lining his forehead.

A smile of abject female joy slowly crossed her face. He saw it and groaned. Captured her mouth with his and pushed her onto her back, coming over the top of her in a position of pure male dominance. For once it didn't scare her. Because in that moment she felt a sense of feminine power she'd never known she had. And it was exhilarating. Drugging. *Freeing.*

'Hook your legs around my waist,' he instructed gruffly.

She did, and immediately felt the smooth rounded head of his penis at her entrance. Totally caught up in the wonder of it, she dug her hands into the small of his back as she pulled him closer.

He hesitated and for a moment her old fear returned, her nerves tightening in anticipation of possible pain, and then he nudged her so sweetly her breath rushed out on a sob. She clasped his head and brought his mouth down to hers, tears burning the backs of her eyes as he slowly eased inside her body.

She easily accommodated him at first, but then she did feel too full. Too stretched.

'Relax, *amada*,' he crooned against her lips. 'I've got you.'

He kissed her hungrily and withdrew almost all the way, before slowly pushing forward again, his tongue filling her mouth and mimicking his lower body's movements until Aspen felt as if she was melting into the bed.

He raised his face above hers and he looked intense. Focused. 'You feel amazing.'

He adjusted his weight and Aspen moaned, arching towards him.

'But you're so tight. I feel like I'm hurting you.'

'No.' She flexed her hips and rubbed against him, gasping as she felt him lodge deeper. 'It feels sensational. *You* feel sensational.'

Cruz groaned and seemed to praise God as he started moving inside her, his strokes smooth and slow before gradually picking up pace. Every time his big body pushed into hers Aspen clung harder to his damp shoulders, her body growing tighter and tighter until with a sudden pause she felt another rush of liquid heat, right before her body convulsed into a paroxysm of pleasure.

Dimly she was aware of Cruz still moving inside her, of her pleasure being completely controlled by the powerful movements of his. And it was endless as he drove into her, over and over and over, until with a pause of his own he tilted her bottom and surged into her with controlled power. Once, twice more, until she cried out and felt him rear his head back and fall over the edge with her.

Again time seemed endless as Aspen stared at the ceiling, slowly coming back into her body. She felt wonderful. Blissfully, sinfully wonderful. Her body was a sweaty, sensual mass of completion. Her hand lifted to Cruz's hair and she caressed the silky strands, enjoying his harsh breaths sawing in and out against her neck.

A smile curved her mouth as she recalled the moment Cruz had guided her hand between her legs so she could feel how wet she was. And she had been. Unbelievably wet—and soft. It had been like touching somebody else's body.

Unbidden, Chad's drunken taunts came to mind and she realised that it had been he who was unable to perform, not her. Deep down, and in moments of total confidence, she had told herself that exact thing, but believing it to be true was something else entirely. Especially when he was such a gregarious and charming person when he wasn't drinking. He was like a Jekyll and Hyde character, she realised, but after tonight what had happened in the bedroom with him would never haunt her again. She wouldn't let it.

Hours later Cruz woke and used the remote console beside his bed to open the curtains. The sky was pale blue outside so he knew it wasn't much after dawn.

Slightly disturbed by the whirring sound of the drapes, Aspen snuggled deeper beneath the covers he'd pulled over them both some time during the night.

Cruz's arm tightened around her shoulders. Last night had blown his mind. First finding out that Aspen had clearly had a poor excuse of a sex-life before him, and second, realising that *he* had had a poor excuse of a sex-life before her. Hell, he'd never come so hard or so often as he had last night, and he was half expecting to be rubbed raw.

He glanced at her delicate features softened by sleep. Her rosy cheeks and the dark sweep of her lashes. He grew hard just thinking about last night.

One night.

He frowned as their deal slid back into his mind like an insidious serpent. Her damned document. At the time one night had seemed like more than enough. He'd thought she was a vacuous princess type he had once lusted after and needed to get out of his system. He'd thought he'd take her to bed, slake his lust for her and move on.

Of course he'd still move on, but…

He thought about the hotel he'd planned to build on Ocean Haven. Last night he'd given up on that plan and, surprisingly, he didn't care. Aspen had been as much a victim of Charles Carmichael's warped ideas about what was right and wrong as he had been—maybe more so.

And the truth was he didn't need Ocean Haven and she did. Ergo, she should have it. Which seemed to be what her uncle thought as well, because he was still obstinately refusing Lauren's increasing offers on Cruz's behalf. He

smiled. Stubborn old goat—he might not be as sanctimo-
nious as his old man, but he'd inherited that attribute from
him, all right.

And good for him—because as soon as Cruz got up he
would tell Lauren to pull out of that particular race. Aspen
had won and for once he didn't mind losing. One day he'd
share that with Ricardo. Have a laugh. One day when he
understood it better.

But for now he had to face facts.

Fact one: Aspen would want to return to Ocean Haven
some time soon. Fact two: he was supposed to be flying
to China to check out the site of the first of his—what was
it?—fifty new hotels first thing tomorrow. Fact three…

Fact three was that he wanted neither of those things to
happen. Fact four was that he didn't know why that was,
and fact five was that she felt divine curled up against his
side. Fact six was that he was definitely going crazy because he was yapping to himself again.

His throat felt as if he had a collar and tie around it.

Previously, making sure that he was rolling in money
had been all that he could think about. He'd put his polo career on hold indefinitely to achieve it. After he'd left Ocean
Haven he could have picked up any number of wealthy
patrons who would have happily paid any fee to have him
play for them, but he would still have been at their beck
and call. Still disposable. Still an outsider in a world of
rank and privilege. So he'd worked hard to change that.
And, although many might say he had now achieved his
goal, pride—or maybe that old sense of being vulnerable—drove him onwards.

But was it enough now? Hadn't he started to question
how much satisfaction he actually derived from pushing
himself so hard? Hadn't that old feeling of wanting a family started poking into his mind again? Wasn't that one
of the reasons he'd tried not to visit his own family? And

here was fact seven: he hated that feeling of being the one left out. Maybe Aspen was right about that. Maybe if he became more human around his family they might be the same with him.

Madre de Dio.

He was doing it again.

Cruz closed his eyes and let himself absorb the slender length of the woman who was pleasantly draped over his side like a human rug. Gently, so as not to disturb her, he stroked her hair. She shifted and the rustle of the sheets carried her scent to his nose. She smelled good. Superb.

His mind conjured up how she had looked last night, spread out beneath him while he made her come with his mouth. His body hardened and he had to bite back a groan. He wasn't sure he could do it again, and he was damned sure she was probably too sore, but his body had other ideas.

Trying to stanch the completely normal reaction of his body to the closeness of a naked woman, Cruz carefully extricated himself from under Aspen's warm body. Better he get up now, have a shower and start the day. It was going to be a busy one. First a round of meetings to finalise what he hadn't done yesterday, and then the polo matches would start just before lunch and run till the afternoon.

He would have made it too—except Aspen chose that moment to move again and attached herself to him like scaffolding on a building site. She moaned and smoothed her hand over his chest.

Cruz had closed his eyes, his senses completely focused on the southerly trajectory of her hand, when she suddenly snatched it back.

'I'm sorry. I…' She sat up and pushed the tangled mass of curls back from her face.

Fact eight: she looked adorable when she woke up. All

soft and pink, with her lips still swollen from where they had ravaged each other.

Unable to help himself, he dropped his eyes to her chest and she gave a small squeak, quickly dragging the sheet up over her nakedness. But not before he'd had a good glimpse of creamy breasts that wore grazes from his beard growth.

For some reason her obvious distress eradicated his own desire to put as much distance between them as possible. Which was surprising when he recalled how he had opened up about his childhood last night. That alone should have had him eating dust. But her loser ex had done her a disservice when it came to intimacy, and Cruz wasn't about to make that worse because he had itchy feet.

'Good morning.'

She turned wild eyes up at him. Dampened her lips. 'Good morning.'

Silence lengthened between them and Cruz realised he had no idea what to say. This was the equivalent of a one-night stand and, while he'd never had what could be considered a long-term relationship, he didn't indulge in one-night stands either.

'This is—'

'Awkward?'

She let out a shaky breath. 'Yes, but last night was…'

'Wonderful.'

She pulled a pained face. 'You don't have to say that. I mean yes, it was good, great for me but…oh, never mind.'

Cruz felt a well of rage at Anderson for hurting her. He wanted to reassure her that he was actually being honest, but he suspected she'd see his words as hollow.

'Spend the day,' he found himself saying instead.

'Why?' Her shocked eyes flew to his and he made sure his own surprise at his invitation didn't show on his face. But why shouldn't she spend the day? He had a first-rate polo tournament starting in a few hours. She loved polo. She ran a horse stud.

'I thought you were busy today?' she said.

'I am.' Her reserved response had him putting the brakes on the surge of pleasure he'd experienced at the thought of her staying with him. 'But there's plenty for you to stay for. The polo, for one. It's going to be an incredible event.'

She gave him a wan smile that made his teeth want to grind together. 'I don't want to complicate things.'

Confused by his own reaction to her reticence, he took refuge in annoyance. 'And how is watching a polo tournament complicating things?'

'Our deal—'

'Forget the deal.' He got out of bed. 'Stay because you want to. Stay because the sun is shining and because there's going to be a world-class polo tournament here that's sold out to the general public. Stay because you work too hard and you need a break.'

'Well, when you put it like that...'

Torn between wanting to kiss her and sending her home, Cruz nearly rescinded his offer when the cell phone on his bedside table rang.

They both looked at it.

'What's your decision?'

She dampened her lips. 'Yes, okay, I'd like to watch the polo.'

Aspen stood on the penthouse balcony and stared out over the shiny green polo field. Horse floats, white marquees, riders, grooms, horse-owners and hotel employees scurried about as they readied themselves for the day ahead.

Yet despite the heady anticipation in the air that preceded a major event all Aspen could think about was what she was still doing here.

Replaying their awkward morning-after conversation in her head, she cringed. When Cruz had first asked her to stay Aspen had felt her heart jump in her chest at the thought of spending the day with him. Then he'd confirmed that he'd be busy and she'd felt like an idiot. Of course he was busy. He had invited her to watch the polo, not to spend the day with *him*.

When his phone had rung she had automatically said yes because he'd looked beautiful and sleep-tousled and she hadn't wanted to leave.

Now she didn't think she could leave fast enough.

Because last night had changed her. She felt it deep within her bones. Last night had been everything she'd ever dreamed making love could be, because Cruz had taken the time to make it that way for her and she could already feel herself wanting to make more out of it than it was. Wanting to make it special, somehow. But what woman *wouldn't* want to do that when she'd just been so completely loved by a man like Cruz Rodriguez?

No, not loved, she quickly amended. Pleasured.

God.

She buried her forehead against her arms, which were resting on the balustrading.

It was beyond clear that Cruz had asked her to stay out of politeness or—worse—pity. She, of course, had said yes out of desire. Desire to spend more time with him. Desire to experience his lovemaking again. Desire to re-experience the pleasure she felt sure only he could give her.

But he was as much of a Jekyll and Hyde character as Chad when it came down to it, because he had come to Ocean Haven specifically to try and take her farm.

She had forgotten that. *Again.*

Was she a glutton for punishment? Was she so used to having men control her that she'd gladly fall in with the plans of another self-interested, power-hungry male?

Because while Cruz might have shown her the best night of her life, it didn't change the reality of why she was even here.

'Forget the deal,' he'd all but snarled.

Last night she had. This morning it was impossible to do so in the cold light of day.

Or course last night she had been in the grip of a wonderful sense of feminine power with Cruz that could easily become addictive if she let it. A smile curved her lips, only to fade away just as quickly. Cruz had freed her from years of feeling as if there was something wrong with her and she'd be forever indebted to him for that. He was also trying to buy her home out from under her, and that was like a sore that wouldn't heal. If she stayed today it would be for the wrong reasons. It would be because she was hoping for more from him. Something she didn't want from any man. Did she?

Aspen groaned. How could she even think about staying longer under the shade of such conflicting emotions?

The simple answer was that she couldn't. And dwelling on it wasn't going to make it any different.

Decision made, she spun on her heel and went to pack her suitcase.

Cruz looked up, annoyed, as his PA opened the door to his meeting. It was taking him all that he had to concentrate as it was, without yet another irritating interruption.

'What is it, Maria?'

He frowned as he heard Aspen's hasty, 'It's okay…don't interrupt…' in the background.

Maria glanced over her shoulder. 'Ah, Señorita Carmichael wishes to speak with you.'

'Send her in.'

Aspen materialised in the doorway and Cruz saw her suitcase by the side of the door.

He frowned harder. 'What's going on?'

'I can see you're busy.' She threw a quick glance around the room at his executive team. 'It can wait.'

'No, it can't.' He pinned her with a hard look, unaccountably agitated as he registered her intention to leave him. 'Is something wrong?'

'No, no. I just came to say goodbye. I didn't want to leave without letting you know I was going.'

'I thought you had decided to stay?'

She swallowed. 'Our deal was concluded this morning and—'

Cruz swore. 'I thought I'd already told you to forget the deal. It's not relevant. I'm not going to buy Ocean Haven any more. It's yours free and clear.'

A myriad of emotions crossed her lovely face, not completely unlike the morning when he had first told her that he *was* going to challenge her for The Farm.

Disbelief, shock, wariness, a tentative joy…

Three days ago he wouldn't have conceived of giving up something he wanted as much as he had wanted Ocean Haven, but a lot had changed in three days. He'd found out the truth about the night he'd left The Farm and he'd made love to Aspen. Held her in his arms all night. Woken with her still in his arms in the morning. When he looked at her he felt things he'd never felt for any woman before her. Feelings he was still unable to categorize.

'Really?' She took a hesitant step towards him. 'You're serious? It's mine?'

'Yes,' he said gruffly, wondering why it was that he couldn't look at her without wanting to strip her clothes off.

'Oh, Cruz…'

She looked as if she might cry, and just when he was about to back away she gave a gurgle of laughter and rushed over to him, jumping up to wind her arms around his neck. Instinctively Cruz grasped the backs of her thighs, and it seemed completely natural to raise her legs and lock them around his hips.

In an instant the chemistry between them ignited and he filled his hands with her taut curves as he sought to steady them both.

'Thank you, thank you… This means so much to me. You have no idea.'

Before he could formulate a sane response she leant forward and kissed him, her silky tongue sneaking out to wrap around his. Cruz held in a groan and took charge of the kiss. This was what he'd wanted from the minute he'd woken up this morning.

Then he'd held himself back. Now, with her honeyed taste on his tongue, he didn't bother. Her mouth was the greatest aphrodisiac he'd ever known.

She moved her hips and Cruz pressed himself more snugly against the seam of her jeans. She murmured something and he almost ignored it, but the words 'We're not alone…' and 'Everyone is watching…' somehow permeated his addled brain.

He glanced around at his stunned executive team. She was right. Not one of them had looked away and he couldn't say he blamed them. He was just as shocked that he'd forgotten they were still in the room as they were at seeing him with a woman locked in his arms.

He released a careful breath.

'Excuse me, everyone. I'm going to have to adjourn this meeting. Again.'

He held Aspen as still as a statue until the door snicked closed. Then he devoured her, pulling at her clothes and unzipping his jeans. He shoved aside the laptop on the mahogany table and laid her down. Her shirt was open around her and her breasts were heaving against the delicate cups of her plain white bra. She looked wild and wanton, her hair spilling out of the French braid she had secured it in.

His hands skimmed her, claimed her, and she arched up off the table towards him.

'That door isn't locked,' she got out between gasps of pleasure.

'No one will come through it unless they want to start looking for a new job.'

'This is…'

'Madness?' His hands felt clumsy as he yanked her jeans down her legs. 'You need to start wearing skirts more,' he complained.

She let out a husky laugh, and then her breath hitched as he ripped her panties aside and parted her legs. She was already slick and ready and he growled his appreciation.

'I've never wanted a woman as much as I want you.'

He ducked his head down and bathed her silky wetness with his tongue. Her legs fell further apart and he saw her watching him as he licked and sucked on her sweetness. The picture of his dark head nestled between her creamy thighs nearly unmanned him, and when he felt her inner walls start to tremble with her imminent release he rose up and pulled her towards the edge of the table.

'Not without me, *mi gatita*. I want to feel you come around me.'

Quickly applying a condom, Cruz hooked her legs over his forearms and drove into her. Her gasp was raw and shocked and, given everything she had revealed to him last night, he tried to check himself.

'No, don't stop. Please.'

Her hands clutched his forearms, urging him closer, and Cruz closed his eyes and pumped himself into her, grazing her clitoris with his thumb to maximise her pleasure. She came hard and fast at exactly the moment he did. Pleasure turned him inside out. The world might have ended at that moment and he wouldn't have had a clue.

CHAPTER TEN

'YOU DO MISS IT.'

'What?'

'Playing polo.'

'What makes you say that?'

'Oh, I don't know.' Aspen smiled up at Cruz. 'The wistful look on your face right now, perhaps.'

They were leaning on the fence post of one of the stable yards, watching the grooms and riders put the finishing touches to their horses before the main tournament got under way.

'I'm assessing the state of the horses.'

Aspen cocked her head and studied his profile, shadowed from the sun by a baseball cap. His hair curled sexily at the sides. 'Why did you give it up?'

He turned his head, his black eyes piercing. 'Money.'

'Ah. I'm sensing there's a theme here.' She laughed.

'No theme,' Cruz growled without heat. 'I didn't have much when I left Ocean Haven and I knew that polo wasn't going to give me what I needed.'

Aspen nodded. 'Money gives you the security that Ocean Haven gives me, but it's our loss. Watching you play polo was like watching poetry in motion.'

He looked at her strangely and then gave her a small smile. 'Those days are long gone now. And, while I did miss it, my life is full enough as it is. By the way...' His

tone turned serious. 'Anderson is here. He was injured
last month in Argentina so he wasn't expected to turn up.
I told him to keep away from you.'

Aspen reeled. So it *had* been Chad she had glimpsed last
night in the hotel foyer. She sucked in a deep breath and
let it out slowly. She hadn't seen him in years, and while
she really didn't want to she didn't want Cruz feeling as
if he had to defend her just because she had unexpectedly
opened up to him.

'You don't have to fight my battles for me, Cruz.'

He shook his head as if he knew better and tapped the
tip of her nose affectionately. 'Somebody has to.' He took
off his cap and fitted it to her head. 'You need a hat if
you're going to stay out in the sun, *mi gatita*. Excuse me
for a minute.'

He headed off inside the stable, his long stride and
two-metre frame seeming to strike sparks in the air as
he moved. Aspen tried to feel annoyed at his high-hand-
edness, but after last night and then this morning on his
conference table it was hard to stay irritated with him over
anything. It had been so long since she had felt this good.

So long since she had just enjoyed herself without the
pressure of work and bills getting in the way.

So long since she had felt the freedom of truly being in
charge of her own destiny.

And it was exhilarating. She grinned to herself. Almost—but not quite—as exhilarating as feeling Cruz move
inside her body. She smiled again. Almost as exhilarating as feeling his mouth on her breasts, between her legs.

As soon as she had *that* thought liquid heat turned her
insides soft and her smile widened, because now that she
recognised the sensation she could actually feel herself
growing moist. She glanced around surreptitiously, just
to make sure no one else could see that she was turning
herself on.

Her newly awakened desire was like a runaway train. And while part of her knew she should probably try and put the brakes on it, another part of her wanted to roll around in it like a cat in the sun.

Mi gatita. His kitten.

Aspen rolled her eyes. She shouldn't get so much joy out of the pet name but she did.

Her cell phone beeped an incoming message and she snatched it out of her pocket, hoping it was her uncle returning her call. Earlier she had left an excited message on his answering machine, informing him that she had raised the money they had agreed upon for her to buy The Farm. She wondered if he had got it yet and whether he was surprised, wishing she could have told him in person. Unfortunately a trip to England was not in the cards for her in the next twenty-five hours. Although, seventy-two hours ago she would have said a trip to Mexico wasn't, either.

Checking her phone, she saw it was just Donny, informing her that he'd organised for Matty, one of the local teenagers who attended her riding school, to relieve him for the day. Aspen quickly texted back to tell him to have a great day off with his family.

Family...

That sounded so nice.

'Catch.'

Cruz's voice broke her reverie and Aspen looked up just in time to grab the bundle of clothes he had tossed at her and to see a smirk on his handsome face. 'What's this?'

'You're my new groom. How soon can you change?'

Aspen didn't miss a beat. 'Five minutes.'

'See Luis over there?' Cruz pointed with his free hand towards the players' area.

'Yes.'

'Meet me there in two.'

Aspen felt deliriously happy. She reached out and grabbed

his arm as he made to walk past, a thrill of excitement racing through her. 'You're really going to play?'

He paused, cocked his head. 'You wanted to see poetry in motion, didn't you?'

Aspen shook her head, smiling at his cockiness.

It was dangerous to feel this much happiness because of a pair of jeans and a shirt, but it wasn't that. It was the man.

She'd fallen in love with him, she realised with a sinking feeling.

He must have sensed her regard because he turned and met her gaze.

'One minute left,' he drawled.

Totally in love, she thought, and she had no idea what to do about it.

He was in love.

The thought gripped him by the throat in the middle of the game just as he was about to make a nearside forehand shot and he nearly fell off his horse and landed on his behind. Fortunately years of training and a horse that could play blind saw him come out of the offensive strike still in the saddle.

He pulled up and let one of his team members carry the ball to the goalposts.

He couldn't be in love with her. It was impossible. He didn't want to be in love with anyone. Not yet. It wasn't part of his plan.

Surely it was just the exhilaration of being out on the polo field again that was sending weird magnetic pulses to his brain? The sense of fun he hadn't felt in far too long?

He glanced towards the players' area and his eyes effortlessly zeroed in on Aspen standing beside one of his players. She wore his Rodriquez Polo cap and her flyaway blond curls billowed out at the sides. She'd put on his team colours and she looked curvy and edible as she clapped her hands wildly.

The horn went, signalling the end of the game, and Cruz trotted towards her almost hesitantly.

Unaware of his thoughts, she beamed up at him. 'You are such a show-off. Congratulations on the win.'

He returned her smile. She was gorgeous. Gorgeous and smart and funny and hot-headed. And, yes, he was in love with her.

Other players thumped him on the back and congratulated him and he could hear the commentators waxing lyrical about his statistics and his comeback—not that this *was* a comeback, more a hiatus in his normal working life—but he wasn't really paying attention to anything other than Aspen.

He hadn't had any idea that he was falling in love with her but now that he had acknowledged it, it made perfect sense. Probably he had always loved her.

And he couldn't wait to tell her because last night and earlier, when he should have been concentrating on work, she had looked at him in such a way that he was confident she felt the same as he did.

Not that he would tell her here. He'd do it in private. Maybe over an elaborate dinner. He smiled, already anticipating the moment.

Aspen took Bandit's reins and he dismounted. 'That last goal was simply brilliant.'

'I thought so.'

He readjusted his helmet and Aspen automatically pushed some of his hair out of his eyes. 'You need a haircut,' she admonished.

He stilled, his gaze holding hers. 'I have something I need to tell you.'

'What is it?'

'Not here.' He shook his head. 'I promised Ricardo I'd

check in with the Chinese delegation I have apparently neglected all day. How about we meet back in the suite in thirty minutes?'

'This sounds serious.'

'It is. Here, let me take Bandit back to the stables for Luis to get her cleaned up.' He mounted and reached down for the mallet Aspen was holding for him. Instead of taking it he gripped her elbow, raised her onto her toes and kissed her soundly. 'Very serious.'

Aspen watched Cruz canter back towards the stables, her fingers pressed to her throbbing lips.

'Now, that was really touching.'

Aspen swung around at the sound of a mocking voice behind her. For a moment all she could do was stare blankly, her mind frozen as if she'd just been zapped.

'Chad,' she finally managed to croak out.

His smile was charming and boyish. 'One and the same, babe, one and the same.'

CHAPTER ELEVEN

HOPING CHAD WAS just an apparition, Aspen blinked rapidly and then gave a sharp gasp as her vision cleared and she saw him properly. 'What happened to your eye?'

He fingered the puffy purple skin of his eye socket. 'I ran into your *boyfriend*. Didn't he tell you?'

Yes, he had, but he'd neglected to say that he'd done anything but talk to him. A warm glow spread through Aspen's torso. As much as she abhorred violence, the fact that Cruz had reacted on her behalf did make her feel good. Special.

'Are you okay?'

'Do you care?' he sneered.

'Of course.' Memories flooded in, preventing her from saying anything else. The unexpectedness of seeing him causing her heart to beat heavily in her chest.

He stood before her, the typical urban male, with his designer haircut, stubble and trendy sportswear. She knew it took him hours to achieve that casually dishevelled appearance, and that he'd always hated the fact that she didn't pay more attention to her own appearance.

'Can't you straighten your hair sometimes? It's a mess.'

'I didn't expect to see you so far from Ocean Haven.'

His words snapped her attention back to him and slowly she started breathing properly again.

'I'm...here on...business.' She stumbled over the words

and furtively looked around for Cruz. Then she felt angry with herself. She was no longer the naïve eighteen-year-old girl who had mistaken friendship for love and had thought that wealth was synonymous with decency. She didn't *need* Cruz to protect her. She didn't need any man to do that.

'Some digs,' Chad continued, looking back at the hotel. 'The stable boy has come a long way.'

'What do you want, Chad?'

'To say hello.'

'Well, now you've said it, so…'

'What?' He held his hands wide as if in surprise. 'That's all you're going to say?'

'We haven't spoken for a long time. I don't see any point in changing that.'

'What if I do?'

Aspen felt her mouth tighten. 'I believe Cruz told you not to come near me.' And she hated pulling that card.

Chad's lip curled. 'See, Boy Wonder would like to think he controls everything, but he doesn't control me. Does he control you, Assie?'

Aspen's mouth tightened. There was no way she was playing mind games with her ex-husband again. She'd done that enough when they had been married.

'Goodbye, Chad.'

She turned on her heel, intent on walking away from him. but it seemed he had other ideas.

'Aspen, wait.' He jogged after her. 'I didn't mean to upset you.'

'No?'

'No. I wanted to apologise to you, actually.'

Aspen stopped. 'For…?'

'For being such an idiot when we got married. I was in a bad way and—'

Aspen held up her hand like a stop sign. 'Don't, Chad.' She knew his game. She had heard his apologies a thousand times before. Usually they amounted to nothing. 'It doesn't matter anymore.' And amazingly it didn't. Cruz had seen to that.

Cruz who was *nothing* like Chad. Cruz who was proud, but gentle. Cruz who was smart and masterful and possessive. And it thrilled her. *He* thrilled her. And she couldn't wait to see him. Maybe even to tell him that she loved him if she had the courage.

She looked at Chad now. Really looked at him. He couldn't hurt her anymore and it made her feel a little giddy.

'Chad, I'm sorry, but I don't want to see you or talk to you. Whatever you have to say is irrelevant.' She smiled inwardly as she borrowed one of Cruz's favourite expressions.

'I just want to be friends, Aspen, put things behind us.'

Aspen felt petty in refusing him, but he had hurt her too much for her ever to consider him as a friend. 'I'd like to put things behind us too, but we can't ever be friends, Chad.'

'Because of *Rodriguez*?' Chad sneered. 'He won't want you for long. His heart belongs to his horses and nothing else.'

Aspen shook her head. This was the Chad she knew too well.

'Is it serious between you?'

'That's none of your business.'

'You're in love with him.' Chad spat on the ground. 'You always were.'

'I wasn't. I thought I loved you.'

'But you didn't, did you? It was him all along. I told your grandfather. That night.'

Aspen frowned. 'It was you who sent him out after me?'

'I watched you chase him like one of his fawning groupies. Did you have sex with him? Your grandfather would never say.'

God, this was awful, but Aspen wasn't sure if she was more appalled that he had talked to her grandfather so intimately about her or that he was talking to her about it now.

'Why do you hate Cruz so much?' She couldn't help asking.

Chad shrugged and stared at her mulishly. 'He was an arrogant SOB who never saw me as competition. He never took me seriously except where you were concerned.'

Aspen gave a sharp, self-conscious laugh. 'And there I was, thinking that you wanted Ocean Haven.'

Chad shook his head. 'I didn't. But he did. And he's won that too, I hear.'

An uneasy sensation slipped down Aspen's spine and she told herself to ignore him. To walk away. 'What is that supposed to mean?'

He looked at her like a hyena scenting a wounded animal. 'Boy Wonder bought The Farm. Not literally—unfortunately—but… You didn't know?'

Aspen knew better than most not to listen to anything Chad said, not to place any importance on his words, but she couldn't make herself leave. Not with her mother's cautionary advice that if something looked too good to be true it usually was ringing loudly in her ears.

'How would you know anything about the sale of The Farm?'

'My daddy wanted to buy it. He had high hopes of swooping in at the last minute and picking it up for a song.'

Aspen's head started to hurt. 'Well, it's not true. Cruz hasn't bought Ocean Haven. Your father has his facts wrong.'

Chad shrugged. 'I guess the guy brokering the deal is the one who has it wrong. My father did wonder when he heard Rodriguez had paid more than double the value of the property.'

More than double?

Aspen felt a burning sensation in the back of her throat. 'Yes, I'd say he's wrong. Excuse me.'

She pushed past Chad, only to have him grab her arm.

'He's not worth it, you know. You can't see it, but he won't hang around for long.'

Hardly in the mood for any more of Chad's snide comments, Aspen turned on him sharply. 'That's not your business, is it?'

Chad reeled back and covered the movement with a disbelieving laugh. 'You've changed.'

'So I've been told.'

She said the words automatically but Aspen knew that if there was any truth to Chad's words then she hadn't changed at all. Because if Cruz had bought The Farm out from under her it would mean that she had fallen into the same trap she had in the past—wanting the love and affection of a man who wouldn't think twice before walking all over her.

Telling herself to calm down, she stabbed the button on the lift to the penthouse and used the temporary access card Cruz had given her.

Chad had admitted that he hated Cruz, so this could just be trouble he was stirring up between them. But how would he know it would cause trouble? He couldn't. No one knew about the private deal she had struck with Cruz. No one but her knew that this morning Cruz had promised her he had decided not to buy Ocean Haven.

Calm, Aspen, she reminded herself, desperately trying to check her temper.

When the lift doors opened her eyes immediately fell on an immaculately dressed woman who looked like a supermodel.

For a minute she thought she was in the wrong suite, but deep down she knew she wasn't.

'I'm sorry…' She frowned. 'I'm looking for Cruz.'

'He's in the shower,' the woman said.

Was he, now?

Aspen swallowed down the sudden feeling of jealousy. The woman was dressed, for heaven's sake. 'And you are…?'

The woman held out her hand. 'I'm Lauren Burnside. Cruz's lawyer. Would I be right in assuming that you're Aspen Carmichael?'

The fact that his lawyer knew of her wasn't a good sign in Aspen's mind. 'Yes. Would *I* be right in assuming you're here about the sale of Ocean Haven?'

The lawyer's eyes flickered at the corners and an awkward silence prevailed over the room. 'You would have to ask Cruz about that.'

Cruz, not Mr Rodriguez, Aspen noted sourly. How well did this woman know him? And why did the thought of this woman running her hands all over Cruz's naked body hurt her so much?

Because you love him, you nincompoop.

Aspen moved to the side table beside the Renoir and placed her hands lightly on the wood-grained surface. Memories of the last time she had stood in this exact position, with Cruz behind her, kissing her neck, murmuring tender words of encouragement to her, lanced her very soul. Yes, she loved him—and that just took this situation from bad to completely hideous.

'His heart belongs to his horses and nothing else.'

Chad getting inside her head did nothing to stave off her temper either. But still she tried to convince herself that she didn't know the facts. That she wouldn't jump to conclusions as Cruz had done about her eight years ago.

'Lauren. Aspen!'

Aspen turned as Cruz entered the room. Pleasure shot through her at the sight of him fresh from the shower in worn jeans and a body-hugging white T-shirt.

He smiled at her.

She looked away, but he had already transferred his attention to the other woman.

'You have the contracts?'

'Right here.'

Aspen turned and leant against the side table, blocking all memories of the intimacies they had shared, blocking the pain of his betrayal, her foolish feelings for him.

'They would be the contracts to finalise the sale of my farm?' she said lightly.

Cruz's eyes narrowed and Aspen knew. She *knew*!

'When were you going to tell me?'

Her casual tone must have alerted him to her state of mind because he didn't take his eyes off her. 'Can you excuse us, please, Lauren?'

'Of course. I'll leave the contracts on the table.'

She threw Cruz an intimate glance and Aspen felt her cheeks heat at having witnessed it.

'So, here we are, then...' Aspen strolled across the room and stopped beside the urn of flowers on the dining table. She stroked the soft rose petals and thought how impervious they were to the fact that she felt like hoisting them up and hurling them across the room.

'Yes. And to answer your earlier question I was going to surprise you over dinner.'

Surprise her? Aspen's mouth hit the floor and her temper shot through the roof. *Surprise her!*

'Dinner? *Dinner?*' She laughed harshly. 'You filthy, gloating bastard.'

'Aspen—'

'Don't.' Disappointment coalesced into rage and she just needed to get away from him. 'Don't say a word. I don't want to hear it. I don't want to hear anything from you. I hate you.'

She whirled away and would have walked out of the room—no, run out of the room—but he was on her in a second.

'Aspen, let me explain.'

'No.' She shoved against him and beat her fists against his chest in her anger. 'You tricked me. You lied to me. You told me you weren't trying to buy Ocean Haven any more but you were.'

'Dammit, Aspen.' He bound her wrists in one of his hands but she broke loose and tried to slap him. 'Stop it, you little hellcat. Dammit. *Ow!* Listen to me. I left a message for Lauren to pull the pin on the sale but she didn't get it,' he said, breathing hard.

As suddenly as her rage had swept over her it left her, and Aspen felt deflated and appalled that she had hit him. She *hated* violence. 'Let me go, Cruz,' she said flatly.

He frowned down at her. 'It's the truth.'

Aspen sighed and pushed away from him, feeling shivery and cold when he released her. 'It doesn't matter.'

'Of course it matters.' Cruz moved to the table and picked up the wad of paper Lauren had left behind. 'Look at this.'

Aspen glanced at it warily. 'What is it?'

'As soon as I found out that your uncle had accepted my offer I had Lauren organise the immediate transfer of the deeds into your name. It's all here in this contract.'

'What?'

'That was what I was going to tell you over dinner.'

Aspen frowned. 'So you're saying our deal is still on?'

Cruz glowered at her. 'Of *course* the deal is not still on. I don't expect you to pay me back. I'm giving you the property.'

'You're giving…' She shook her head. 'You mean lending me the money to buy it?'

'No, I mean giving it to you.'

'Why would you do that?'

'Because this way you have security.'

'Security?'

'You would have been bankrupt within the year if you'd borrowed all that money.'

Scowling, she moved away from him. 'That's not true. I have a great business plan to get Ocean Haven out of trouble and—' She stopped as he shook his head at her as if she didn't have a clue.

'Aspen, there's no way you can carry that kind of debt and survive,' he said softly.

His words registered in her brain as if she was sitting at the back of a large lecture theatre and trying to read off a tiny whiteboard. 'So you're just giving it to me?'

'It's just a property, Aspen.'

It's just a dress.

It's just her self-worth.

Just her *heart*.

'I don't want you to give it to me,' she said.

'Why are you being so stubborn about this?'

Why? She didn't know. And then she did. For years she'd thought that all she wanted was security, but really—really what she wanted was validation. Trust in her judgement. What she wanted was to know that she could direct her own future. Her way. But somewhere in the last couple of days Cruz had become the centre of her world. Just as both her grandfather and Chad had been at one stage.

Hadn't she once pinned her hopes and dreams for the future on both of them and been let down?

She shook her head. 'I don't want it that way.'

'What way? *Hell!*' Cruz raked a hand through his hair. 'I don't see what the problem is.'

'I want to do it my way.'

'So do it your way,' he almost roared in frustration. 'Debt-free.'

'I would have thought you of all people would understand,' she said, completely exasperated. 'You hated that your mother didn't trust you to do things your way when you were a teenager.'

'This is not that same thing.'

'It is to me.'

'You're being stupid now.'

Aspen rounded on him. 'Do not call me stupid. I had one man put me down. I won't take it from another.'

'*Dios mio*, I didn't mean it like that.' He turned his back on her and then swung back just as quickly. 'Aspen, I'm in love with you.'

Aspen wrapped her arms around her chest as if she was trying to hold her heart in. Was this some backhanded way for him to get Ocean Haven? She stared at him, her emotions in turmoil, a terrible numbness invading her limbs.

'You're not.'

Cruz swore. 'I've just spent over two hundred million dollars on a property I'm prepared to give you. What would you call it?'

'Crazy.'

'Well, it is that…'

'What would you buy me for my birthday?' she asked suddenly.

Cruz frowned. 'Your birthday is…two months away.'

'You have no idea, do you?'

'How is that relevant?'

It was relevant because she knew if he presented her with an envelope full of cash it would break her heart. It was relevant because if he really loved her for who she was he *would* have some idea.

His eyes narrowed on her face. 'What is this? Some kind of test?'

'And if it is?'

A calmness seemed to pervade his limbs. 'You're being ridiculously stubborn about this. I'm giving you everything that you want. Most women would be on their knees with gratitude right now.'

Aspen wasn't sure if he meant sexually, but the fact that she thought it startled her. She wanted to be on her knees in front of him. She wanted to do all sorts of things to his body until he was as out of control as she was. But that wasn't right. His power over her was so much stronger than Chad's. Or her grandfather's. If she stayed, if she accepted his *gift*, she knew she would do anything for him. Would accept anything from him. And that scared her to death. She would be completely at his mercy and a shadow of herself. A woman seeking the approval of a man who didn't listen to her. It wasn't how she wanted to live her life. Nor was he the type of person she wanted to share her life with. Not again.

'I don't play those games, Aspen,' he warned.

'And I don't play yours. Not anymore. Goodbye, Cruz. I hope you never run out of money. You'll be awfully lost if you do.'

Thankfully the lift doors opened just as she pressed the button, but it wasn't divine intervention finally looking out for her. Ricardo was inside. His wide smile of greeting faltered when he glimpsed her expression and a stilted silence filled the space between them as she waited for the lift doors to close.

Once they had, Ricardo turned to his brother. 'What was that all about?'

Cruz let out a harsh laugh. 'That was Aspen Carmichael making me feel like a fool. Again.'

CHAPTER TWELVE

EXACTLY ONE WEEK to the day later Cruz sat on the squash court beside his brother after a particularly gruelling game. Both of them were sweat-soaked and exhausted and Cruz relished the feeling of complete burnout that had turned his muscles to rubber.

His phone beeped an incoming message and since he was right there he checked it.

Frustration warred with disappointment when he saw that it was from Lauren Burnside. Well, what had he expected? Aspen Carmichael to send him a message telling him how much she missed him?

Right. She'd rejected him. How many ways did he need to be kicked before he got the message?

'Now the woman sends me a text,' he muttered.

'Who?'

'My lawyer.'

Maybe if she'd dropped in he would have taken her up on her offer to get up close and personal with his abs. He wouldn't mind losing himself in a woman right now. Smelling her sweet floral scent with a touch of vanilla. Winding his hands through her tumble of wild curls. Hearing her laugh.

'You're muttering,' Ricardo said unhelpfully.

That was because he needed to visit a loony bin so that he could undergo electroshock therapy and once and for all convince his body that Aspen Carmichael was *not* the woman to end all women. Bad enough that he'd thought he had been in love with her. That he'd told her.

He clamped down on the unwanted memory. It had been a foolish thought that had died as soon as she'd walked out through the door. A foolish thought brought on by an adrenaline rush after the polo match.

Feeling spent, he scrolled through Lauren's text. 'Idiot woman.'

'I thought she looked quite smart.'

'Not Lauren. Aspen.'

'Ah.'

Cruz scowled. 'This is not a dentist, *amigo*. Close your mouth.'

Ricardo smiled. 'Are you going to tell me what she'd done now?'

'According to Lauren, she's signed Ocean Haven over to me.'

'Shouldn't you be happy about that? I mean, isn't that what you wanted?'

'No.' He ignored the interested expression on his brother's face. 'I don't want anything to do with that property ever again.' Scowling, he punched a number into his phone. 'Maria, get the jet fuelled up and cancel any meetings I have later today.'

'I thought you just said you didn't want anything to do with that property ever again?'

'I won't after I handle this.'

'Ah, *hermano*, I hate to point out the obvious, but this didn't end so well for you last week.'

Cruz picked up his bag and shoved his racquet inside. 'Last week I was too attached to the outcome. I'm not now.'

Aspen was in a wonderful mood. Super, in fact. Her chores were almost done for the day and all that was left was to bed Delta down in her stall. Now that the polo season was over there was less pressure on her and Donny to have the place ready for Wednesday night chukkas and there were fewer students. That was a slight downside, but Aspen found that as winter rolled around the lessons veered more towards dressage, with her students preferring to practise in the indoor arena rather than get frostbite in the snow.

Pity about the leak.

'Or not,' she said, to no one in particular. Roofs and their holes, walls and their peeling paint, fences and their rusted nails were no longer her problem. And she couldn't be happier.

'Ow!' Aspen glanced down at her thumb and winced. 'Damn thing.'

She looked at her other fingers with their newly bitten nails. When had that happened? When had she started biting her nails again? She hadn't since she was about thirteen and her grandfather had painted that horrible-tasting liquid on the ends of them.

Rubbing at the small wound, she picked up the horse rug she planned to throw over Delta and headed for her stall.

Delta whickered.

'Hello, beauty,' Aspen crooned. 'I see you've finished dinner. Me? I'm not hungry.'

Which was surprising, really, because she couldn't remember if she'd even eaten that day.

'Who needs food anyway?' She laughed. Who needed food when you didn't have any will to live? 'Now, that's not true,' she told Delta. 'I have plenty to live for. Becoming a vet, a new beginning, adventure, never having to see Cruz Rodriguez ever again.'

She leant against the weathered blanket she'd tossed over Delta's back. He'd told her he loved her but how could you love someone you didn't know? And she'd nearly convinced herself that she had loved him too.

'It's called desire,' she informed the uninterested mare. 'Lust that is so powerful it fries your brain.'

But she wasn't going to think about that. Had forbidden herself to think about it all week. And it had worked. Sort of.

Aspen took in a deep breath and revelled in the smell of horse and hay and Ocean Haven. Her throat constricted and tears pricked at the back of her eyes, her energy suddenly leaving her. She would miss this. Miss her horses. Her school. But things changed. That was the only certainty in life, wasn't it?

'The man who now owns you is big and strong and he'll take care of you.' Delta tossed her head. 'I'm serious. He loves horses more than anything else.'

'Is that right?'

Aspen spun around. Stared. Then swallowed. Cruz stood before her, wearing a striking grey suit and a crisp white shirt. 'What are you doing here?'

'I think you know why I'm here this time.'

She straightened her spine. 'Boy, that lawyer of yours works fast.'

'She should. She's paid enough. Now, answer my question.'

Aspen straightened Delta's already straight blanket over her rump. Better that than looking at Cruz and losing her train of thought. 'I would have thought it was obvious. You bought Ocean Haven so it's yours, not mine.'

'I told you that was a mistake,' he bit out. 'The whole thing happened while I was playing polo.'

Aspen shook her head. 'You really expect me to believe that?' she scoffed. 'That supermodel of yours wouldn't blink without your say-so.'

'Supermodel?'

'We *are* talking about the brunette who happened to know you were in the shower, aren't we?'

Cruz narrowed his gaze and Aspen stared him down. Then he smiled. A full-on toothpaste-commercial-worthy smile. 'I've never slept with Lauren.'

'Like I would care.' She jerked her head. 'Mind moving? I'm tired of you blocking my way. No pun intended.'

Cruz continued to smile. 'None taken.'

But he didn't move.

'You're right about Lauren acting under my instructions,' he began. 'Unfortunately they were my *old* instructions. My *new* ones were caught up somewhere in cyberspace when her firm's e-mail system went down.'

'I don't care. I'm moving on.'

'Where to?'

'I don't know.' She shrugged. 'Somewhere exciting.'

'And what about your mother's horseshoe?'

'It's gone.' She'd cried over that enough when she'd returned last week. 'And before you ask I don't know where and nor does Donny. When I came back last week it wasn't here.' She sniffed. 'I'm taking it as a sign.'

'A sign of what?'

His voice was soft. As gentle as it had been the night she had told him about Chad. It made a horrible pain well up inside her chest. 'A sign that I've put too much store in The Farm for too long. I thought I needed it, but it turns out I needed something else more.'

He stepped closer to her. 'What?'

'It's irrelevant. You know what *that* means, don't you, Cruz?'

Unfortunately he ignored her blatant dig. Blast him.

'Try me.'

'No.' She moved away from him and fossicked with Delta's feed bucket. 'I've discovered that I do have some pride after all, so...no.'

Cruz grabbed the feed bucket and took it out of her numb fingers. Aspen accidentally took a deep breath and it was all him. When he took her hands she closed her eyes to try and ward off how good it felt to have him touch her. She swallowed. Yanked her hands out of his.

'I'm going to finish my vet course and take an internship somewhere, start over,' she said quickly.

Not taking the hint that she didn't want him to touch her, he slid his hand beneath her chin and raised her eyes to his. 'Start over with me?'

Aspen jerked back. 'I didn't know you were looking for a new vet?'

'I don't mean professionally and you know it,' he growled. Then his voice softened. 'I've missed you, *mi gatita*. I love you.'

'I—'

'You don't believe me?' He blew out a breath. 'Kind of ironic that a week ago it was me who didn't believe you, wouldn't you say?'

Aspen's chest felt tight. 'No. I wouldn't.' Nothing seemed ironic to her right now. More like tragic.

Cruz pushed a hand through his hair and Aspen wished he was a thousand miles away. So much easier to deny her feelings when he wasn't actually right beside her.

'I know you're angry, Aspen, and I don't blame you. I thought I knew about human nature. I thought I had it all covered. But you showed me I was wrong. After your grandfather kicked me out I vowed never to need anyone again. I saw money as the way to ensure that I was never expendable. I was wrong. I understand why you didn't want me to give you The Farm now, and if you want we'll consider it a loan. You can pay me back.'

Aspen felt a spurt of hope at his words. But that didn't change their fundamental natures. She couldn't afford to be in love with him. She'd become needy for his affection and he'd do it again. At some point he wouldn't listen to her and they'd be right back where they started. Better to save herself that pain now.

'I can't.'

'I know you were hurt, Aspen. By your grandfather's expectations, by the lucky-to-still-be-breathing Anderson. Me. But I promise if you give me a chance I won't hurt you again.'

Aspen shook her head sadly. 'You will.' Her cheeks were damp and Cruz brushed his thumbs over the tears she hadn't even known she was shedding. 'You won't mean to, because I know deep down you're kind-hearted, but—' She stopped. Recalled what she had said to Delta. He *would* take care of her. But could she trust his love? Could she trust him to listen to her in the future? Could she trust that she wouldn't get lost in trying to please him? 'I'm not great in relationships.'

'Then we really are perfect for each other because I'm hopeless. Or at least I was. You make me want to change all that. You make me feel human, Aspen. You make me want to *embrace* life again.'

Aspen's nose started tingling as she held back more useless tears.

'I know you're scared, *chiquita*. I was too.'

'Was?' She glanced at him.

Cruz leaned towards her and kissed her softly. 'Was.' He gave a half smile and reached inside his jacket pocket. He pulled out a small red velour pouch. 'You asked me last week what I would get you for your birthday and I had no idea. It took me a while, but finally I realised that I was imposing my way of fixing things over yours.'

Aspen gazed at the small pouch he'd placed in her hand.

'One of my flaws is that I see something wrong and I want to fix it. My instinct is to take care of those around me. The only way I knew how to do that without getting hurt was to remain emotionally detached from everything.

But no matter how hard I tried I couldn't do that with you. You fill me up, Aspen and you make me feel so damned much. You make me want so much. No one else has ever come close.'

Aspen's mouth went dry as she felt the hard piece of jewellery inside the pouch. She'd guessed what it was already and she honestly didn't know what her response should be. She wanted to be with Cruz more than anything else in the world but the ring felt big. Huge, in fact. Oh, no doubt it would be beautiful, but it wouldn't be *her*. It wouldn't be something she would ever feel comfortable wearing—especially with her job—and it was just one more sign that they could never make a proper relationship work.

'Open it. It's not what you think it is.'

Untying the drawstrings with shaky fingers, Aspen carefully tipped the contents of the pouch into her hand.

'Oh!' Her breath whooshed out of her lungs and she stared at a tiny, delicate wood carving of a horse attached to a thin strip of leather. 'Oh, Cruz, its exquisite.' Her shocked eyes flew to his. 'It's just like the ones I saw lined up on your mother's mantelpiece. You *did* do them for her, didn't you?'

'I did,' he confirmed gruffly.

Studying him, she was completely taken aback by the raw emotion on his face and her lips trembled as her own deep feelings broke to the surface. 'You *do* love me.'

Cruz cupped her face in his hands and lifted her mouth to his for a searing kiss. 'I do. More than life itself.'

'Oh.' Aspen clutched Cruz's shoulders and welcomed the fold of his strong embrace as the hot tears she had been holding at bay spilled recklessly down her cheeks. 'You've made me cry.'

'And me.'

Aspen looked up and found that his eyes were wet. She

touched a tear clinging to the bottom of his lashes. 'When did you make this?'

'During the week. I couldn't concentrate on anything and my executive team were just about ready to call in the professionals with white coats. I have to say it took a few attempts before my fingers started working again.'

Aspen clutched the tiny horse. 'I'll treasure it.'

'And I'll treasure you. Turn around,' he commanded huskily.

Aspen let out a shaky breath, happiness threatening to burst right out of her. She clasped the tiny horse to her chest as he gently moved her hair aside and tied the leather strap around her neck. Then she turned back to face him.

He looked down to where the horse lay nestled between her breasts. 'You do know that in some countries this binds you to me for ever?'

Aspen smiled. 'For ever?'

'Completely. And in case you're at all unsure what I mean by that I have something else.'

He produced a small box and Aspen knew this time it would be a ring. She also knew that no matter how ostentatious it was she would accept it from him, because she knew it had come from a place of absolute love.

Smiling, she opened it and got the third shock of the day. Inside, nestled on a bed of green silk, was the most exquisitely formed diamond ring she had ever seen. And by Cruz's standards it must have seemed—

'It's tiny! Oh, I'm sorry.' She clapped her hand over her mouth. 'That came out wrong.'

Cruz grimaced and slid the beautiful ring onto her finger. 'It wasn't my first choice, believe me, but I knew if I got you anything larger you'd think it was impractical.'

Aspen laughed and flung herself into his arms, utter joy flooding her system at how well he *did* know her. 'I love it!'

Cruz grunted and then lifted her off the ground and

kissed her. 'I'm getting you matching diamond earrings next, and they're so heavy you won't be able to stand up.'

'Then I'll only wear them in bed.' Smiling like a loon, she rained kisses down all over his face. 'Oh, Cruz, it's perfect. *You're* perfect.'

'So does that mean you're going to put me out of my misery and tell me you love me? Because I know you do.'

'How do you know that?'

'You called my lawyer a supermodel.'

Aspen pulled back. 'You think I was jealous of her?'

'I hope so. Now, please, *mi chiquita*, say yes and become indebted to me for the rest of your life?'

'You'll really lend your wife money and let her pay you back?'

'If she ever gets around to telling me that she loves me I'll let her do whatever she wants, as long as she promises to only do it with me.'

'Yes, Cruz.' Aspen nuzzled his neck and basked in the sensation of safety and love that enveloped her. 'I love you and I will be indebted to you for the rest of my life.'

Cruz touched the tiny horse that lay between her breasts. 'And I you, *mi gatita*. And I you.'

* * * * *

Mills & Boon® Hardback
January 2014

ROMANCE

The Dimitrakos Proposition	Lynne Graham
His Temporary Mistress	Cathy Williams
A Man Without Mercy	Miranda Lee
The Flaw in His Diamond	Susan Stephens
Forged in the Desert Heat	Maisey Yates
The Tycoon's Delicious Distraction	Maggie Cox
A Deal with Benefits	Susanna Carr
The Most Expensive Lie of All	Michelle Conder
The Dance Off	Ally Blake
Confessions of a Bad Bridesmaid	Jennifer Rae
The Greek's Tiny Miracle	Rebecca Winters
The Man Behind the Mask	Barbara Wallace
English Girl in New York	Scarlet Wilson
The Final Falcon Says I Do	Lucy Gordon
Mr (Not Quite) Perfect	Jessica Hart
After the Party	Jackie Braun
Her Hard to Resist Husband	Tina Beckett
Mr Right All Along	Jennifer Taylor

MEDICAL

The Rebel Doc Who Stole Her Heart	Susan Carlisle
From Duty to Daddy	Sue MacKay
Changed by His Son's Smile	Robin Gianna
Her Miracle Twins	Margaret Barker

Mills & Boon® Large Print
January 2014

ROMANCE

Challenging Dante — Lynne Graham
Captivated by Her Innocence — Kim Lawrence
Lost to the Desert Warrior — Sarah Morgan
His Unexpected Legacy — Chantelle Shaw
Never Say No to a Caffarelli — Melanie Milburne
His Ring Is Not Enough — Maisey Yates
A Reputation to Uphold — Victoria Parker
Bound by a Baby — Kate Hardy
In the Line of Duty — Ami Weaver
Patchwork Family in the Outback — Soraya Lane
The Rebound Guy — Fiona Harper

HISTORICAL

Mistress at Midnight — Sophia James
The Runaway Countess — Amanda McCabe
In the Commodore's Hands — Mary Nichols
Promised to the Crusader — Anne Herries
Beauty and the Baron — Deborah Hale

MEDICAL

Dr Dark and Far-Too Delicious — Carol Marinelli
Secrets of a Career Girl — Carol Marinelli
The Gift of a Child — Sue MacKay
How to Resist a Heartbreaker — Louisa George
A Date with the Ice Princess — Kate Hardy
The Rebel Who Loved Her — Jennifer Taylor

Mills & Boon® Hardback

February 2014

ROMANCE

A Bargain with the Enemy	Carole Mortimer
A Secret Until Now	Kim Lawrence
Shamed in the Sands	Sharon Kendrick
Seduction Never Lies	Sara Craven
When Falcone's World Stops Turning	Abby Green
Securing the Greek's Legacy	Julia James
An Exquisite Challenge	Jennifer Hayward
A Debt Paid in Passion	Dani Collins
The Last Guy She Should Call	Joss Wood
No Time Like Mardi Gras	Kimberly Lang
Daring to Trust the Boss	Susan Meier
Rescued by the Millionaire	Cara Colter
Heiress on the Run	Sophie Pembroke
The Summer They Never Forgot	Kandy Shepherd
Trouble On Her Doorstep	Nina Harrington
Romance For Cynics	Nicola Marsh
Melting the Ice Queen's Heart	Amy Ruttan
Resisting Her Ex's Touch	Amber McKenzie

MEDICAL

Tempted by Dr Morales	Carol Marinelli
The Accidental Romeo	Carol Marinelli
The Honourable Army Doc	Emily Forbes
A Doctor to Remember	Joanna Neil

0114GEN STD HB

Mills & Boon® *Large Print*
February 2014

ROMANCE

The Greek's Marriage Bargain	Sharon Kendrick
An Enticing Debt to Pay	Annie West
The Playboy of Puerto Banús	Carol Marinelli
Marriage Made of Secrets	Maya Blake
Never Underestimate a Caffarelli	Melanie Milburne
The Divorce Party	Jennifer Hayward
A Hint of Scandal	Tara Pammi
Single Dad's Christmas Miracle	Susan Meier
Snowbound with the Soldier	Jennifer Faye
The Redemption of Rico D'Angelo	Michelle Douglas
Blame It on the Champagne	Nina Harrington

HISTORICAL

A Date with Dishonour	Mary Brendan
The Master of Stonegrave Hall	Helen Dickson
Engagement of Convenience	Georgie Lee
Defiant in the Viking's Bed	Joanna Fulford
The Adventurer's Bride	June Francis

MEDICAL

Miracle on Kaimotu Island	Marion Lennox
Always the Hero	Alison Roberts
The Maverick Doctor and Miss Prim	Scarlet Wilson
About That Night...	Scarlet Wilson
Daring to Date Dr Celebrity	Emily Forbes
Resisting the New Doc In Town	Lucy Clark

Mills & Boon® Online

Discover more romance at
www.millsandboon.co.uk

- **FREE** online reads
- **Books** up to one month before shops
- **Browse our books** before you buy

...and much more!

For exclusive competitions and instant updates:

 Like us on **facebook.com/millsandboon**

 Follow us on **twitter.com/millsandboon**

 Join us on **community.millsandboon.co.uk**

Visit us Online | Sign up for our FREE eNewsletter at **www.millsandboon.co.uk**

WEB/M&B/RTL5/HB